TOLD UNDER THE GREEN UMBRELLA

He holds a green umbrella over the good children, and then they dream the most delightful stories all night long.

—*Olé Luköié.*

TOLD UNDER THE GREEN UMBRELLA

Old Stories for New Children

Selected by the

LITERATURE COMMITTEE OF THE
INTERNATIONAL KINDERGARTEN UNION

Pictures by GRACE GILKISON

NEW YORK
THE MACMILLAN COMPANY
1937

TO
THE CHILDREN OF TODAY
FROM
THE CHILDREN OF YESTERDAY

CONTENTS

CONTENTS

LIST OF ILLUSTRATIONS

TOLD UNDER THE GREEN UMBRELLA

OLÉ LUKÖIÉ, THE DUSTMAN

THERE is nobody in all the world who can tell so many stories as Olé Luköié! And such stories as he can tell!

When night is drawing on, and the children are sitting round the table as good as possible or on their little footstools, in walks Olé Shut-eyes. He comes so quietly up the stairs without his shoes, and opens the door so softly that nobody hears him; and, puff! he sends a shower of milk into their eyes in such fine spray as to be invisible; but they can't keep their eyes open after it, and so they never see him. He steals behind them and breathes upon their necks, making their heads as heavy as lead. But he never hurts them; he

1

does it all from kindness to the children. He only wants them to be quiet, and the best way to make them quiet is to have them in bed; when they are settled there, he can tell them his stories.

Then as soon as the children are asleep, Olé Luköié seats himself upon their beds. He is well dressed; his clothes are all of silk, but it is impossible to say what color they are, for it shimmers green, red, and blue every time he turns. He has a green umbrella under his arm, with pictures on it, and this he holds over the good children, and then they dream the most delightful stories all night long. The other umbrella has no pictures on it, and he holds this one over the children who have been naughty, and then they sleep heavily till the morning and have no dreams at all.

I am now going to tell you about a little boy to whom Olé Luköié went. His name was Hjalmar. He told him this story on a Thursday, so it is called the Thursday story.

"I'll tell you what!" said Olé Luköié. "Don't be frightened, and I will show you a little mouse." And he stretched out his hand with the tiny little animal in it. "It has come to invite you to a wedding. There are two little mice who intend to enter the wedded state to-night. They live under the floor of your mother's larder, which they say is a most delightful residence."

"But how can I get through a little mouse hole in the floor?" said Hjalmar.

"Leave that to me," said Olé Luköié, "I'll soon make you small enough!"

Then he touched Hjalmar with his wand, and he quickly grew smaller and smaller; at last he was not as tall as one's finger.

"Now you may borrow the tin soldier's clothes; I think they'll just fit you, and it looks so smart to have on a uniform when one's in company."

"Yes indeed!" said Hjalmar, and in a moment he was dressed like the grandest tin soldier.

"Be so good as to take a seat in your mother's thimble," said the little mouse, "and I shall have the honor of drawing you!"

"Heavens! Are you going to take that trouble yourself, young lady?" said Hjalmar, and off they drove to the mouse's wedding.

First they went down under the floor into a long passage, which was just high enough for them to drive through, and the whole passage was lighted up with touchwood.

"Isn't there a delicious smell here?" said the mouse who was drawing him. "The whole passage has been smeared over with bacon fat! Nothing could be nicer."

Then they came to the bridal hall, where all the little lady mice stood on the right whispering and giggling, as if they were making fun of each other, and on the left stood all the gentlemen mice stroking their whiskers with their paws. The bridal pair stood in the middle of the room, in the hollow rind of a cheese, kissing each other most energetically before all the other people; but then they were engaged, you know, and just about to be married.

More and more visitors poured in, the mice were almost crushing each other to death, and the bridal pair had taken their place in the doorway, so that one could neither get in nor out. The whole room, like the passage, was smeared with bacon fat; there were no other refreshments, but for dessert a pea was produced in which one of the little mice of the family had bitten the name of the bridal pair—that is to say, the first letter of it; and this was something quite extraordinary. All the mice said it was a delightful wedding, and the conversation most entertaining.

And then Hjalmar drove home again; he had been in very grand company, but in order to get there he had been obliged to shrink wonderfully, to make himself small enough to get into the uniform of a tin soldier.

THE THREE LITTLE PIGS

ONCE upon a time there was an old Sow with three little Pigs, and as she had not enough to keep them, she sent them out to seek their fortune.

The first that went off met a Man with a bundle of straw, and said to him, "Please, Man, give me that straw to build me a house." Which the Man did, and the little Pig built a house with it. Presently came along a Wolf, and knocked at the door, and said, "Little Pig, little Pig, let me come in."

To which the Pig answered, "No, no, by the hair of my chinny chin chin."

"Then I'll huff and I'll puff, and I'll blow your house in!" said the Wolf. So he huffed and he puffed, and he blew his house in, and ate up the little Pig.

The second Pig met a Man with a bundle of furze, and said, "Please, Man, give me that furze to build a house." Which the Man did, and the Pig built his house. Then along came the Wolf and said, "Little Pig, little Pig, let me come in."

"No, no, by the hair of my chinny chin chin."

"Then I'll puff and I'll huff, and I'll blow your

house in!" So he huffed and he puffed, and he puffed and he huffed, and at last he blew the house down, and ate up the second little Pig.

The third little Pig met a Man with a load of bricks, and said, "Please, Man, give me those bricks to build

a house with." So the Man gave him the bricks, and he built his house with them. So the Wolf came, as he did to the other little Pigs, and said, "Little Pig, little Pig, let me come in."

"No, no, by the hair of my chinny chin chin."

"Then I'll huff and I'll puff, and I'll blow your house in."

Well, he huffed and he puffed, and he huffed and he puffed, and he puffed and he huffed; but he could *not* get the house down. When he found that he could not, with all his huffing and puffing, blow the house down, he said, "Little Pig, I know where there is a nice field of turnips."

"Where?" said the little Pig.

"On, in Mr. Smith's home field; and if you will be ready to-morrow morning, I will call for you, and we will go together and get some for dinner."

"Very well," said the little Pig, "I will be ready. What time do you mean to go?"

"Oh, at six o'clock."

Well, the little Pig got up at five, and got the turnips and was home again before six. When the Wolf came he said, "Little Pig, are you ready?"

"Ready!" said the little Pig. "I have been and come back again, and got a nice potful for dinner."

The Wolf felt very angry at this, but thought that he would be *up to* the little Pig somehow or other; so he said, "Little Pig I know where there is a nice apple tree."

"Where?" said the Pig.

"Down at Merry-garden," replied the Wolf; "and

if you will not deceive me I will come for you, at five o'clock to-morrow, and we will go together and get some apples."

Well, the little Pig woke at four the next morning, and bustled up, and went off for the apples, hoping to get back before the Wolf came; but he had farther to go, and had to climb the tree, so that just as he was coming down from it, he saw the Wolf coming, which, as you may suppose, frightened him very much. When the Wolf came up he said: "Little Pig, what! are you here before me? Are they nice apples?"

"Yes, very," said the little Pig; "I will throw you down one." And he threw it so far that, while the Wolf was gone to pick it up, the little Pig jumped down and ran home.

The next day the Wolf came again, and said to the little Pig, "Little Pig, there is a Fair in the Town this afternoon: will you go?"

"Oh, yes," said the Pig, "I will go; what time shall you be ready?"

"At three," said the Wolf.

So the little Pig went off before the time, as usual, and got to the Fair, and bought a butter churn, and was on his way home with it when he saw the Wolf coming. Then he could not tell what to do. So he got into the churn to hide, and in doing so turned it round;

and it began to roll, and rolled down the hill with the Pig inside it, which frightened the Wolf so much that he ran home without going to the Fair.

He went to the little Pig's house, and told him how frightened he had been by a great round thing which came down the hill past him.

Then the little Pig said: "Hah! I frightened you, did I? I had been to the Fair and bought a butter churn, and when I saw you I got into it, and rolled down the hill."

Then the Wolf was very angry indeed, and declared he *would* eat up the little Pig, and that he would get down the chimney after him.

When the little Pig saw what he was about, he hung on the pot full of water, and made up a blazing fire, and, just as the Wolf was coming down, took off the cover of the pot, and in fell the Wolf. And the little Pig put on the cover again in an instant, boiled him up, and ate him for supper, and lived happy ever after.

THE PANCAKE

ONCE on a time there was a woman who had seven hungry children, and she was frying a pancake for them. It was a sweet milk pancake, and there it lay in the pan, bubbling and frizzling so thick and good, it was a delight to look at it. And the children stood round about, and the old father sat by and looked on.

"Oh, give me a bit of pancake, mother dear, I am so hungry," said one child.

"Oh, darling mother," said the second.

"Oh, darling, good mother," said the third.

"Oh, darling, good sweet mother," said the fourth.

"Oh, darling, pretty, good, sweet mother," said the fifth.

"Oh, darling, pretty, good, sweet, clever mother," said the sixth.

"Oh, darling, pretty, good, sweet, clever, kindest little mother," said the seventh.

So they begged for the pancake all around, the one more prettily than the other, for they were so hungry and so good.

"Yes, yes, children, only bide a bit till it turns itself"

(she ought to have said, "till I can get it turned"), "and then you shall have some lovely sweet milk pancake. Only look how fat and happy it lies there."

When the pancake heard all this it became afraid, and in a trice it turned itself and tried to jump out of the pan, but it fell back into it again, the other side up. When it had been fried a little on the other side too, till it got firm and stiff, it jumped out of the pan to the floor and rolled off like a wheel through the door and down the hill.

"Holloa! Stop, pancake!" And away ran the mother after it, with the frying pan in one hand and the ladle in the other, as fast as she could, and all the children behind her, while the old father on crutches limped after them last of all.

"Hi! Won't you stop? Catch it! Stop, pancake!" they all screamed out, one after another, and tried to catch it on the run and hold it. But the pancake rolled on and on, and in a twinkling of an eye it was so far ahead that they couldn't see it.

So when it had rolled awhile it met a man.

"Good day, pancake," said the man.

"Good day, Manny Panny!" said the pancake.

"Dear pancake," said the man, "don't roll so fast; stop a little and let me eat you."

"No, no; I have run away from the mother, and the

father, and seven hungry children. I'll run away from you, Manny Panny," said the pancake, and it rolled and rolled till it met a hen.

"Good day, pancake," said the hen.

"The same to you, Henny Penny," said the pancake.

"Pancake, dear, don't roll so fast. Bide a bit and let me eat you up," said the hen.

"No, no; I have run away from the mother, and the father, and seven hungry children, and Manny Panny. I'll run away from you, too, Henny Penny," said the pancake, and it rolled on like a wheel down the road.

Just then it met a cock.

"Good day, pancake," said the cock.

"The same to you, Cocky Locky," said the pancake.

"Pancake dear, don't roll so fast, but bide a bit and let me eat you up."

"No, no; I have run away from the mother, and the father, seven hungry children, Manny Panny, and Henny Penny. I'll run away from you too, Cocky Locky," said the pancake, and it rolled and rolled as fast as it could. By and by it met a duck.

"Good day, pancake," said the duck.

"The same to you, Ducky Lucky."

"Pancake dear, don't roll away so fast; bide a bit and let me eat you up."

"No, no; I have run away from the mother, and the father, and seven hungry children, Manny Panny, Henny Penny, and Cocky Locky. I'll run away from you, too, Ducky Lucky," said the pancake, and with that it took to rolling and rolling faster than ever; and when it had rolled a long, long while, it met a goose.

"Good day, pancake," said the goose.

"The same to you, Goosey Poosey."

"Pancake dear, don't roll so fast; bide a bit and let me eat you up."

"No, no; I have run away from the mother, the father, seven hungry children, Manny Panny, Henny Penny, Cocky Locky, and Ducky Lucky. I'll run away from you, too, Goosey Poosey," said the pancake, and off it rolled.

So when it had rolled a long way off, it met a gander.

"Good day, pancake," said the gander.

"The same to you, Gander Pander," said the pancake.

"Pancake dear, don't roll so fast; bide a bit and let me have a bite."

"No, no; I've run away from the mother, the father, seven hungry children, Manny Panny, Henny Penny, Cocky Locky, Ducky Lucky, and Goosey Poosey. I'll run away from you, too, Gander Pander," said the pancake, and it rolled and rolled as fast as ever.

So when it had rolled a long, long time, it met a pig.

"Good day, pancake," said the pig.

"The same to you, Piggy Wiggy," said the pancake, and without a word more it began to roll and roll for dear life.

"Nay, nay," said the pig, "you needn't be in such a hurry; we two can go side by side through the wood; they say it is not too safe in there."

The pancake thought there might be something in that, and so they kept company. But when they had gone awhile, they came to a brook. As for Piggy, he was so fat he could swim across. It was nothing for him, but the poor pancake could not get over.

"Seat yourself on my snout," said the pig, "and I'll carry you over."

So the pancake did that.

"Ouf, ouf," said the pig, and swallowed the pancake at one gulp, and then, as the poor pancake could go no farther, why—this story can go no farther either.

THE OLD WOMAN AND HER PIG

AN OLD WOMAN was sweeping her house, and she found a little crooked sixpence. "What," said she, "shall I do with this little sixpence? I will go to market, and buy a little pig."

As she was coming home, she came to a stile: but the piggy wouldn't go over the stile.

She went a little further, and she met a dog. So she said to him: "Dog! dog! bite pig; piggy won't go over the stile; and I shan't get home to-night." But the dog wouldn't.

She went a little further, and she met a stick. So she said: "Stick! stick! beat dog! dog won't bite pig; piggy won't get over the stile; and I shan't get home to-night." But the stick wouldn't.

She went a little further, and she met a fire. So she said: "Fire! fire! burn stick; stick won't beat dog; dog won't bite pig; piggy won't get over the stile; and I shan't get home to-night." But the fire wouldn't.

She went a little further, and she met some water. So she said: "Water! water! Quench fire; fire won't burn stick; stick won't beat dog; dog won't bite pig;

16

*"Dog! Dog! bite pig; piggy won't go over the stile;
and I shan't get home to-night."*

piggy won't get over the stile; and I shan't get home to-night." But the water wouldn't.

She went a little further, and she met an ox. So she said: "Ox! ox! drink water; water won't quench fire; fire won't burn stick; stick won't beat dog; dog won't bite pig; piggy won't get over the stile; and I shan't get home to-night." But the ox wouldn't.

She went a little further, and she met a butcher. So she said: "Butcher! butcher! kill ox; ox won't drink water; water won't quench fire; fire won't burn stick; stick won't beat dog; dog won't bite pig; piggy won't get over the stile; and I shan't get home to-night." But the butcher wouldn't.

She went a little further, and she met a rope. So she said: "Rope! rope! hang butcher; butcher won't kill ox; ox won't drink water; water won't quench fire; fire won't burn stick; stick won't beat dog; dog won't bite pig; piggy won't get over the stile; and I shan't get home to-night." But the rope wouldn't.

She went a little further, and she met a rat. So she said: "Rat! rat! gnaw rope; rope won't hang butcher; butcher won't kill ox; ox won't drink water; water won't quench fire; fire won't burn stick; stick won't beat dog; dog won't bite pig; piggy won't get over the stile; and I shan't get home to-night." But the rat wouldn't.

She went a little further, and she met a cat. So she said: "Cat! cat! kill rat; rat won't gnaw rope; rope won't hang butcher; butcher won't kill ox; ox won't drink water; water won't quench fire; fire won't burn; stick won't beat dog; dog won't bite pig; piggy won't get over the stile; and I shan't get home to-night." But the cat said to her. "If you will go to yonder cow and fetch me a saucer of milk, I will kill the rat." So away went the old woman to the cow.

But the cow said to her: "If you will go to yonder haystack and fetch me a handful of hay, I'll give you the milk." So away went the old woman to the hay-stack; and she brought the hay to the cow.

As soon as the cow had eaten the hay, she gave the old woman the milk; and away she went with it in a saucer to the cat.

As soon as the cat had lapped up the milk, the cat began to kill the rat; the rat began to gnaw the rope; the rope began to hang the butcher; the butcher began to kill the ox; the ox began to drink the water; the water began to quench the fire; the fire began to burn the stick; the stick began to beat the dog; the dog began to bite the pig; the little pig in a fright jumped over the stile; and so the old woman got home that night.

THE THREE BILLY GOATS GRUFF

ONCE on a time there were three Billy Goats, who were to go up to the hillside to make themselves fat, and the family name of the goats was "Gruff."

On the way up was a bridge, over a river which they had to cross, and under the bridge lived a great ugly Troll with eyes as big as saucers, and a nose as long as a poker.

First of all came the youngest Billy Goat Gruff to cross the bridge. "Trip, trap; trip, trap!" went the bridge.

"Who's that tripping over my bridge?" roared the Troll.

"Oh, it is only I, the tiniest Billy Goat Gruff, and I'm going up to the hillside to make myself fat," said the Billy Goat, with such a small voice.

"Now, I'm coming to gobble you up," said the Troll.

"Oh, no! Pray do not take me: I'm too little, that I am," said the Billy Goat. "Wait a bit till the second Billy Goat Gruff comes—he's much bigger."

"Well! be off with you," said the Troll.

A little while after came the second Billy Goat Gruff across the bridge.

"Trip, trap! trip, trap! trip, trap!" went the bridge.

"Who is that tripping over my bridge?" roared the Troll.

"Oh, it's the second Billy Goat Gruff, and I'm going up to the hillside to make myself fat," said the Billy Goat. Nor had he such a small voice, either.

"Now, I'm coming to gobble you up!" said the Troll.

"Oh, no! Don't take me. Wait a little till the big Billy Goat comes; he's much bigger."

"Very well! Be off with you," said the Troll.

But just then up came the big Billy Goat Gruff.

"Trip, trap! trip, trap! trip, trap!" went the bridge, for the Billy Goat was so heavy that the bridge creaked and groaned under him.

"*Who's that tramping on my bridge?*" roared the Troll.

"It's I! the big Billy Goat Gruff," said the Billy Goat and he had a big hoarse voice.

"Now, I'm coming to gobble you up!" roared the Troll.

> "Well come! I have two spears so stout,
> With them I'll thrust your eyeballs out:
> I have besides two great big stones,
> With them I'll crush you, body and bones!"

That was what the big Billy Goat said; so he flew at the Troll, and thrust him with his horns, and crushed him to bits, body and bones, and tossed him out into the river, and after that he went up to the hillside.

There the Billy Goats got so fat that they were scarcely able to walk home again, and if they haven't grown thinner, why, they're still fat; and so—

> "Snip, snap, stout.
> This tale's told out."

SCRAPEFOOT

ONCE upon a time, there were three Bears who lived in a castle in a great wood. One of them was a great big Bear, and one was a middling Bear, and one was a little Bear. And in the same wood there was a Fox who lived all alone; his name was Scrapefoot. Scrapefoot was very much afraid of the Bears, but for all that he wanted very much to know all about them. And one day as he went through the wood he found himself near the Bears' Castle, and he wondered whether he could get into the castle. He looked all about him everywhere, and he could not see any one. So he came up very quietly, till at last he came up to the door of the castle, and he tried whether he could open it. Yes! the door was not locked, and he opened it just a little way, and put his nose in and looked, and he could not see any one. So then he opened it a little way farther, and put one paw in, and then another paw, and another and another, and then he was all in the Bears' Castle. He found he was in a great hall with three chairs in it—one big, one middling, and one little chair; and he thought he would like to sit down and rest and look about him; so he sat down on the big chair. But he found it so hard and uncomfortable that it made his bones ache, and he jumped down at once and got into the middling chair, and he turned round and round in it, but he couldn't make himself comfortable. So then he went to the little chair and sat down in it, and it was so soft and warm and comfortable that Scrapefoot was quite happy; but all at once it broke to pieces under him and he couldn't put it together again! So he got up and began to look about him again, and on one table he saw three saucers, of which one was very big, one was middling, one was quite a little saucer. Scrapefoot was very thirsty, and he began to drink out of the big saucer. But he only just tasted the milk in the big saucer, which was so sour and so nasty that he would not taste another drop of it. Then he tried the middling saucer, and he drank a little of that. He tried two or three mouthfuls, but it was not nice; and then he left it and went to the little saucer, and the milk in the little saucer was so sweet and so nice that he went on drinking it till it was all gone.

Then Scrapefoot thought he would like to go upstairs; and he listened and he could not hear any one. So upstairs he went, and he found a great room with three beds in it; one was a big bed, and one was a middling bed, and one was a little white bed; and he climbed up into the big bed, but it was so hard and lumpy and uncomfortable that he jumped down again at once, and tried the middling bed. That was rather better, but he could not get comfortable in it, so after turning about a little while he got up and went to the little bed; and that was so soft and so warm and so nice that he fell fast asleep at once.

And after a time the Bears came home, and when they got into the hall the big Bear went to his chair and said, "WHO'S BEEN SITTING IN MY CHAIR?" and the middling Bear said, "WHO'S BEEN SITTING IN MY CHAIR?" and the little Bear said, *"Who's been sitting in my chair and has broken it all to pieces?"* And then they went to have their milk, and the big Bear said, "WHO'S BEEN DRINKING MY MILK?" and the middling Bear said, "WHO'S BEEN DRINKING MY MILK?" and the little Bear said, *"Who's been drinking my milk and has drunk it all up?"* Then they went upstairs and into the bedroom, and the big Bear said, "WHO'S BEEN SLEEPING IN MY BED?" and the middling Bear said, "WHO'S BEEN SLEEPING IN MY BED?" and the little Bear said, *"Who's been sleeping in my bed?—and see, here he is!"*

So then the Bears came and wondered what they should do with him; and the big Bear said, "Let's hang him!" and then the middling Bear said, "Let's

They swung him backward and forward, and out of the window.

drown him!" and then the little Bear said, "Let's throw him out of the window." And then the Bears took him to the window, and the big Bear took two legs on one side and the middling Bear took two legs on the other side, and they swung him backward and forward, backward and forward, and out of the window.

Poor Scrapefoot was so frightened, and he thought every bone in his body must be broken. But he got up and first shook one leg—no, that was not broken; and then another, and that was not broken; and another and another, and then he wagged his tail and found there were no bones broken. So then he galloped off home as fast as he could go, and never went near the Bears' Castle again.

THE RACE BETWEEN HARE AND HEDGEHOG

IT WAS once upon a time on a Saturday morning in autumn, while the barley fields were still in bloom.

The sun was shining, the morning wind was blowing over the stubble, the larks were singing high in the air, the bees were buzzing in the barley blossoms, and the people were going blithely about their day's work; in short, all the world was happy, and the Hedgehog, too.

The Hedgehog stood in front of his door with folded arms, looked at the weather, and hummed a tune as only a hedgehog can hum on a Saturday morning.

Now, as he stood there humming, he thought to himself all at once that, while his wife was washing and dressing the children, he might as well go for a little walk in the fields and see how his turnips were getting on.

The turnips grew near his house, and he and his family ate as many of them as ever they wanted, and so he looked upon them quite naturally as his property.

Well, the Hedgehog slammed his door and started

for the turnip field. He hadn't got very far, and was just sauntering round the brier bush that stood outside the field, when he met the Hare, who was out on the same errand—namely, to look at his cabbages.

When the Hedgehog caught sight of the Hare, he gave him a pleasant "Good morning."

But the Hare, who was a very aristocratic person in his own way, and very high and mighty in his manner, didn't answer the Hedgehog's greeting, but said, with a nasty sneer: "What are you running about the fields for so early in the morning?"

"I'm out walking," said the Hedgehog.

"Walking?" grinned the Hare. "I should have thought you could use your legs for something better!"

This remark annoyed the Hedgehog, for, though he was a good-natured fellow enough, he was touchy on the subject of his legs, which were, by nature, bandy.

"I suppose," he said tartly, "you think your legs are better than mine?"

"That I do," said the Hare.

"It remains to be seen," said the Hedgehog. "I bet you that if we two were to run a race I should outstrip you."

"Absurd!" cried the Hare. "You with your crooked legs! But if you're so anxious to try, I've no objection. What do you wager?"

"A golden guinea," said the Hedgehog.

"Done!" said the Hare. "We'll start right away!"

"Oh, don't be in such a hurry," said the Hedgehog. "I haven't had my breakfast yet, and I feel a bit faint. I'll come back here in an hour."

So away he trotted, for the Hare made no objection. Then he thought to himself:

"The Hare thinks a lot of his long legs, but I'll get the better of him all the same. For all his haughty ways, he's not so very clever, and I'll make him pay; see if I don't."

As soon as he got home, he said to his wife:

"Quick! go and get dressed. You must come out with me."

"What's the matter?" said his wife.

"I've wagered the Hare a golden guinea. I'm to run a race with him, and I want you to be there."

"Good gracious me!" cried the Hedgehog's wife. "Have you lost your senses? How can you think of racing the Hare?"

"Don't be so quick with your words, woman," said the Hedgehog. "That's my affair; you mustn't meddle with what you don't understand. Look sharp; put on your things, and come along."

What was the wife to do? She had to obey, whether she wanted to or not.

On the way to the field, the Hedgehog said:

"Now, listen to what I'm going to tell you. In that plowed field over there we're to run our race. The Hare will run in one furrow, and I in the other. We begin at the top. Now, all you've got to do is to stand at the other end of my furrow, and directly the Hare arrives, you call out to him:

"Here I am already!"

With that they reached the field. The Hedgehog told his wife where to stand, and went on to the other end.

The Hare was there waiting for him.

"Shall we start?" asked the Hare.

"Right," said the Hedgehog.

"Now then!"

Each took up his place.

The Hare counted:

"One, two, three!"

And away he went like the wind.

But the Hedgehog took about three paces, then he went back, ducked down in his furrow, and stood there as comfortably as you please, and laughing as if he would split his sides.

Now, the moment the Hare came rushing up to the other end, the Hedgehog's wife called out to him:

"Here I am already!"

The Hare was quite taken aback, for he made sure it was the Hedgehog himself who was sitting there calling to him, since as every one knows, a hedgehog's wife looks exactly like her husband.

"There's something not quite right here," said the Hare. "We must run again back to the starting point."

And away he flew like the wind. But the Hedgehog's wife never moved.

When the Hare got to the other end, the Hedgehog called out:

"Here I am already!"

But the Hare, quite beside himself with jealousy, shouted:

"We must run again!"

"Right!" said the Hedgehog. "As often as you like."

And so the Hare went on, running backward and forward seventy-three times, and every time the Hedgehog got the better of him. Every time the Hare arrived at one end or the other, the Hedgehog or his wife called out:

"Here I am already!"

But the seventy-fourth time the Hare dropped down dead-tired before he got halfway. So the Hedgehog took his golden guinea, and he and his wife went home very well pleased with themselves. And so my tale is finished.

THE SHEEP AND THE PIG THAT
BUILT THE HOUSE

THERE was once upon a time a sheep who stood in his pen to be fattened, so he lived well and every day he had all that he could eat. So it went on until one day, when the dairymaid came to bring him his food, she said:

"Eat away, sheep: you won't be here much longer. To-morrow we are going to kill you."

But the sheep ate until he was ready to burst; and when he had finished he butted out the door of his pen and took his way to the neighboring farm.

There he went straight to the pigsty, where there lived a pig whom he had met out on the common.

"Good day," said the sheep, "and thanks for your kindness the last time we met."

"Good day," said the pig, "and the same to you."

"Do you know why they feed you and make you so comfortable?" said the sheep.

"No," said the pig.

"Because they are going to kill you and eat you," said the sheep.

"Much good may it do them," said the pig.

"If you will come with me," said the sheep, "we will go to the woods and build us a house, and there we can live very comfortably."

Yes, the pig was willing. "Good company is a fine thing," he said, and so the two set off.

When they had gone a bit farther they met a goose.

"Good day, good sirs," said the goose, "and thanks for our last merry meeting. Where are you going to-day?"

"Good day to you," said the sheep. "You must know we were too well treated at home, and so we are going to the woods to build a house for ourselves."

"May I go with you?" said the goose. "For it's child's play when three share the day."

"What can you do to build a house?" said the pig.

"I can pull moss and stuff it in the cracks and make your house tight and warm," said the goose.

Yes, she might go with them, for above all things the pig wished to be warm and comfortable.

So when they had gone a little farther, for the goose found it hard work to keep up with them, they met a hare, who came frisking out of the wood.

"Good day, sirs, and thanks for our last merry meeting. How far are you traveling to-day?" said he.

"Good day, and the same to you," said the sheep.

"We were far too well off at home, and so we are going to the wood to build us a house; for you know there is nothing like home."

"As for that," said the hare, "I have a home in every bush; but yet I have often said in winter, if I only live till summer I'll build me a house; and so I have half a mind to go with you."

"We might take you along to frighten away the dogs," said the pig, "but I don't know what you can do toward building a house."

"There is always work for willing hands," said the hare. "I have teeth to gnaw pegs, and paws to drive them into the wall, so I can very well set up to be a carpenter."

Yes, he too might go with them and help to build the house.

When they had gone a bit farther they met a cock.

"Good day, good sirs," said the cock. "Where are you going to-day, gentlemen?"

"Good day, and the same to you," said the sheep. "At home we were too well off, and so we are going to the woods to build us a house."

"Well," said the cock, "that is just my case. Now, if I might have leave to join such a gallant company, I also would like to go to the woods and build a house."

"After all a home is best," said the sheep.

"How can you ever help us to build a house?" said the pig.

"Oh," said the cock, "I am up early and I can wake every one."

"Very true," said the pig. "Let him come with us."

So they all set off to the wood to build a house. The pig cut down the timber and the sheep drew it home; the hare was carpenter, and gnawed pegs and bolts, and hammered them into the walls and roof; the goose pulled moss and stuffed it into the cracks; the cock crew and looked out that they did not oversleep in the morning. And when the house was ready, and the roof lined with birch bark and covered with turf, there they lived by themselves and were well and merry.

" 'Tis good to travel east and west," said the sheep, "but after all, a home is best."

THE TRAVELS OF A FOX

ONE day a fox was digging behind a stump and he found a bumblebee; and the fox put the bumblebee in a bag and took the bag over his shoulder and traveled.

At the first house he came to he went in and said to the mistress of the house, "May I leave my bag here while I go to Squintum's?"

"Yes," said the woman.

"Then be careful not to open the bag," said the fox.

But as soon as he was out of sight the woman said to herself, "Well, I wonder what the fellow has in his bag that he is so careful about. I will look and see. It can't do any harm, for I shall tie the bag right up again."

However, the moment she unloosed the string out flew the bumblebee, and the rooster caught him and ate him all up.

After a while the fox came back. He took up his bag and knew at once that his bumblebee was gone, and he said to the woman, "Where is my bumblebee?"

And the woman said, "I untied the string just to take a little peep to find out what was in your bag,

The rooster flew out and the pig caught him.

and the bumblebee flew out and the rooster ate him."

"Very well," said the fox; "I must have the rooster, then."

So he caught the rooster and put him into his bag and traveled.

At the next house he came to he went in and said to the mistress of the house, "May I leave my bag here while I go to Squintum's?"

"Yes," said the woman.

"Then be careful not to open the bag," said the fox.

But as soon as he was out of sight the woman said to herself, "Well, I wonder what the fellow has in his bag that he is so careful about. I will look and see. It can't do any harm, for I shall tie the bag right up again."

However, the moment she unloosed the string the rooster flew out and the pig caught him and ate him all up.

After a while the fox came back. He took up his bag and knew at once that his rooster was gone, and he said to the woman. "Where is my rooster?"

And the woman said, "I untied the string just to take a little peep to find out what was in your bag, and the rooster flew out and the pig ate him."

"Very well," said the fox, "I must have the pig, then."

So he caught the pig and put him in his bag and traveled.

At the next house he came to he went in and said to the mistress of the house, "May I leave my bag here while I go to Squintum's?"

"Yes," said the woman.

"Then be careful not to open the bag," said the fox.

But as soon as he was out of sight the woman said to herself, "Well, I wonder what the fellow has in his bag that he is so careful about. I will look and see. It can't do any harm, for I shall tie the bag right up again."

However, the moment she unloosed the string the pig jumped out and the ox gored him.

After a while the fox came back. He took up his bag and knew at once that his pig was gone, and he said to the woman, "Where is my pig?"

And the woman said, "I untied the string just to take a little peep to find out what was in your bag, and the pig jumped out and the ox gored him."

"Very well," said the fox, "I must have the ox, then."

So he caught the ox and put him in his bag and traveled.

At the next house he came to he went in and said to the mistress of the house, "May I leave my bag here while I go to Squintum's?"

"Yes," said the woman.

"Then be careful not to open the bag," said the fox.

But as soon as he was out of sight the woman said to herself, "Well, I wonder what the fellow has in his bag that he is so careful about. I will look and see. It can't do any harm, for I shall tie the bag right up again."

However, the moment she unloosed the string the ox got out, and the woman's little boy chased the ox out of the house and across a meadow and over a hill, clear out of sight.

After a while the fox came back. He took up his bag and knew at once that his ox was gone, and he said to the woman, "Where is my ox?"

And the woman said, "I untied the string just to take a little peep to find out what was in your bag, and the ox got out and my little boy chased him out of the house and across a meadow and over a hill, clear out of sight."

"Very well," said the fox, "I must have the little boy, then."

So he caught the little boy and put him in his bag and traveled.

At the next house he came to he went in and said to the mistress of the house, "may I leave my bag here while I go to Squintum's?"

"Yes," said the woman.

"Then be careful not to open the bag," said the fox.

The woman had been making cake, and when it was baked she took it from the oven, and her children gathered around her teasing for some of it.

"Oh, ma, give me a piece!" said one, and "Oh, ma, give me a piece!" said each of the others.

And the smell of the cake came to the little boy in the bag, and he heard the children beg for the cake, and he said, "Oh, mammy, give me a piece!"

Then the woman opened the bag and took the little boy out; and she put the house dog in the bag in the little boy's place, and the little boy joined the other children.

After a while the fox came back. He took up his bag and he saw that it was tied fast and he thought that the little boy was safe inside. "I have been all day on the road," said he, "without a thing to eat, and I am getting hungry. I will just step off into the woods now and see how this little boy I have in my bag tastes."

So he put the bag on his back and traveled deep into the woods. Then he sat down and untied the bag, and if the little boy had been in there things would have gone badly with him.

But the little boy was at the house of the woman who made the cake, and when the fox untied the bag the house dog jumped out and killed him.

THE ELVES AND THE SHOEMAKER

THERE was once a shoemaker who worked very hard and was honest. Still, he could not earn enough to live upon, and at last all he had in the world was gone except just leather enough to make one pair of shoes. He cut these out at night, and meant to get up early the next morning to make them up.

His heart was light amid all his troubles, for his conscience was clear. So he went quietly to bed, left all his cares to God, and fell asleep. In the morning he said his prayers and sat down to work, when, to his great wonder, there stood the shoes, already made, upon the table.

The good man knew not what to say or think. He looked at the work; there was not one false stitch in the whole job; all was neat and true.

That same day a customer came in, and the shoes pleased him so well that he readily paid a price higher than usual for them. The shoemaker took the money and bought leather enough to make two pairs more. He cut out the work in the evening and went to bed early. He wished to be up with the sun and get to work.

He was saved all trouble, for when he got up in the morning, the work was done, ready to his hand. Pretty soon buyers came in, who paid him well for his goods. So he bought leather enough for four pairs more.

He cut out the work again overnight, and found it finished in the morning as before. So it went on for some time. What was got ready at night was always done by daybreak, and the good man soon was well to do.

One evening, at Christmas time, he and his wife sat over the fire, chatting, and he said:

"I should like to sit up and watch to-night, that we may see who it is that comes and does my work for me."

The wife liked the thought. So they left a light burning, and hid themselves behind a curtain to see what should happen.

As soon as it was midnight there came two little elves. They sat upon the shoemaker's bench, took up all the work that was cut out, and began to ply with their little fingers. They stitched and rapped and tapped at such a rate that the shoemaker was all amazement and could not take his eyes off them for a moment.

On they went busily till the job was quite done, and the shoes stood, ready for use, upon the tables. This was long before daybreak. Then they bustled away as

The shoemaker could not take his eyes off them.

quick as lightning. The next day the wife said to the shoemaker:

"These little elves have made us rich, and we ought to be thankful to them and do them some good in return. I am quite vexed to see them run about as they do. They have nothing upon their backs to keep off the cold. I'll tell you what we must do; I will make each of them a shirt, and a coat and waistcoat, and a pair of pantaloons into the bargain. Do you make each of them a little pair of shoes."

The good shoemaker liked the thought very well. One evening, they had the clothes ready, and laid them on the table instead of the work they used to cut out. Then they went and hid behind the curtain to watch what the little elves would do.

At midnight the elves came in and were going to sit down at their work as usual; but when they saw the clothes lying there for them, they laughed and were in high glee. Then they dressed themselves in the twinkling of an eye, and danced and capered and sprang about as merry as could be, till at last they danced out of the door, and over the green.

The shoemaker saw them no more, but everything went well with him from that time forward as long as he lived.

THE LAD WHO WENT TO THE
NORTH WIND

ONCE on a time there was an old widow who had one son, and as she was feeble and weak, she asked her son to go out to the storehouse and fetch meal for cooking. But when he got outside the storehouse, and was just going down the steps, there came the North Wind, puffing and blowing, caught up the meal, and away with it through the air. Then the lad went back into the storehouse for more; but when he came out again on the steps, the North Wind came again and carried off the meal with a puff; and more than that, he did it the third time. At this the lad got very angry; and as it seemed hard that the North Wind should behave so, he thought he would go in search of him and ask him to give up his meal.

So off he went, but the way was long, and he walked and walked. At last he came to the North Wind's house.

"Good day" said the lad, "and thank you for coming to see us."

"Good day," answered the North Wind, and his voice was loud and gruff, "and thanks for coming to see me. What do you want?"

"Oh," answered the lad, "I only wished to ask you to be so good as to let me have back the meal you took from me on the storehouse steps, for we haven't much to live on; and if you're to go on snapping up the morsel we have, there'll be nothing for it but to starve."

"I haven't your meal," said the North Wind; "but since you are in such need, I'll give you a tablecloth which will get you everything you want. You need only say, 'Cloth, spread yourself, and serve up all kinds of good dishes!'"

With this the lad was well content. But, as the way was long, he could not get home in one day; so he turned into an inn on the way; and when they were going to sit down to supper he laid the cloth on the table which stood in the corner, and said:

"Cloth, spread yourself, and serve up all kinds of good dishes."

He had scarcely said this before the cloth did as it was bid, and all who stood by thought it a fine thing, but most of all the landlord. So, when all were fast asleep, at dead of night, he took the lad's cloth, and put another like it in its stead. But this could not so much as serve up a bit of dry bread.

When the lad woke he took the cloth and went off with it, and that day he got home to his mother.

"Now," said he, "I've been to the North Wind's

house, and a good fellow he is, for he gave me this cloth and when I only say to it, 'Cloth, spread yourself, and serve up all kinds of good dishes,' I get every sort of food I please."

"All very true, I dare say," said the mother, "but seeing is believing."

So the lad made haste, drew out a table, laid the cloth on it and said:

"Cloth, spread yourself, and serve up all kinds of good dishes."

But not even a bit of dry bread did the cloth serve up.

"Well!" said the lad, "there's no help for it but to go to the North Wind again." And away he went.

So, late in the afternoon, he came to where the North Wind lived.

"Good evening!" said the lad.

"Good evening!" said the North Wind.

"I want my rights for that meal of ours which you took," said the lad; "for, as for that cloth I got, it isn't worth a penny."

"I have no meal," said the North Wind; "but you may have the ram yonder which will coin gold ducats when you say to it:

"Ram, ram! Make money!"

The lad thought this a fine thing; but as it was too

"Oh, my! oh, my! Bid the stick be still."

far to get home that day, he turned in for the night to the same inn where he had slept the first time.

Before he called for anything, he tried what the North Wind had said of the ram, and found it all true. When the landlord saw this, he thought it a fine ram, and when the lad had fallen asleep, he took another which could not coin even a penny, and exchanged the two.

Next morning off went the lad, and when he got home to his mother, he said:

"After all, the North Wind is a jolly fellow, for now he has given me a ram, which will coin golden ducats if I only say, 'Ram, ram! Make money!'"

"All very true, I dare say," said his mother, "but I shan't believe it until I see the ducats made."

"Ram, ram! Make money!" said the lad; but not even a penny did the ram coin.

So the lad went back to the North Wind and scolded him, and said the ram was worth nothing, and he must have his rights for the meal.

"Well!" said the North Wind, "I've nothing else to give you but that old stick in the corner yonder; but it's a stick of such a kind that if you say, 'Stick, stick! Lay on!' it lays on till you say, 'Stick, stick! Now stop!'"

So the lad thanked the North Wind and went his

way, and as the road was long, he turned in this night also to the landlord; but as he could guess pretty well how things stood as to the cloth and the ram, he lay down at once on the bench and began to snore, as if he were asleep. Now the landlord who thought surely the stick must be worth something, hunted up one which was like it, and when he heard the lad snore he was going to exchange the two; but, just as the landlord was about to take it, the lad called out:

"Stick, stick! Lay on!"

So the stick began to beat the landlord, till he jumped over chairs and tables and benches, and yelled and roared:

"Oh, my! oh, my! Bid the stick be still, else it will beat me to death. You shall have back both your cloth and your ram."

When the lad thought the landlord had had enough, he said: "Stick, stick! Now stop!"

Then he took the cloth and put it into his pocket, and went home with his stick in his hand, leading the ram by a cord tied around its horns; and so he got his rights for the meal he had lost.

THE STRAW OX

THERE were, once upon a time, an old man and an old woman. The old man worked in the fields as a pitch burner, while the old woman sat at home and spun flax. They were so poor that they could save nothing at all; all their earnings went in bare food, and when that was gone there was nothing left. At last the old woman had a good idea.

"Look, now, husband," cried she, "make me a straw ox, and smear it all over with tar."

"Why, you foolish woman!" said he. "What's the good of an ox of that sort?"

"Never mind," said she, "you just make it. I know what I am about."

What was the poor man to do? He set to work and made the ox of straw, and smeared it all over with tar.

The night passed away, and at early dawn the old woman took her distaff and drove the straw ox out into the steppe to graze, and she herself sat down behind a hillock and began spinning her flax, and cried:

"Graze away, little ox, while I spin my flax; graze away, little ox, while I spin my flax!" And while she spun, her head drooped down, and she began to doze, and while she was dozing, from behind the dark wood and from the back of the huge pines a bear came rushing out upon the ox and said:

"Who are you? Speak and tell me!"

And the ox said:

"A three-year-old heifer am I, made of straw and smeared with tar."

"Oh!" said the bear. "Stuffed with straw and trimmed with tar, are you? Then give me of your straw and tar, that I may patch up my ragged fur again!"

"Take some," said the ox; and the bear fell upon it and began to tear away at the tar.

He tore and tore, and buried his teeth in it till he found he couldn't let go again. He tugged and he tugged, but it was no good, and the ox dragged him gradually off, goodness knows where. Then the old woman awoke, and there was no ox to be seen. "Alas! old fool that I am!" cried she. "Perchance it has gone home." Then she quickly caught up her distaff and spinning-board, threw them over her shoulders, and hastened off home, and she saw that the ox had dragged the bear up to the fence, and in she went to her old man. "Dad, dad!" she cried. "Look, look! the ox has brought us a bear. Come out and kill him!" Then the

"Give me of your straw and tar."

old man jumped up, tore off the bear, tied him up, and threw him in the cellar.

Next morning, between dark and dawn, the old woman took her distaff and drove the ox into the steppe to graze. She herself sat down by a mound, began spinning, and said:

"Graze, graze away, little ox, while I spin my flax! Graze, graze away, little ox, while I spin my flax!" And while she spun, her head drooped down, and she dozed. And, lo! from behind the dark wood, from the back of the huge pines, a gray wolf came rushing out upon the ox and said:

"Who are you? Come, tell me!"

"I am a three-year-old heifer, stuffed with straw and trimmed with tar," said the ox.

"Oh, trimmed with tar, are you? Then give me of your tar to tar my sides, that the dogs and the sons of dogs tear me not!"

"Take some," said the ox. And with that the wolf fell upon it and tried to tear the tar off. He tugged and tugged, and tore with his teeth, but could get none off. Then he tried to let go, and couldn't; tug and worry as he might, it was no good. When the old woman awoke, there was no heifer in sight. "Maybe my heifer has gone home!" she cried; "I'll go home and see." When she got there she was astonished, for by the paling stood the ox with the wolf still tugging at it. She ran and told her old man, and her old man came and threw the wolf into the cellar also.

On the third day the old woman again drove her ox into the pasture to graze, and sat down by a mound and dozed off. Then a fox came running up. "Who are you?" she asked the ox.

"I'm a three-year-old heifer, stuffed with straw and daubed with tar."

"Then give me some of your tar to smear my sides with, when those dogs and sons of dogs tear my hide!"

"Take some," said the ox. Then the fox fastened her teeth in it and couldn't draw them out again. The old woman told her old man, and he took and cast the fox into the cellar in the same way. And after that they caught Pussy Swiftfoot likewise.

So when he had got them all safely the old man sat down on a bench before the cellar and began sharpening a knife. And the bear said to him:

"Tell me, daddy, what are you sharpening your knife for?"

"To flay your skin off, that I may make a leather jacket for myself and a pelisse for my old woman."

"Oh, don't flay me, daddy dear! Rather let me go, and I'll bring you a lot of honey."

"Very well, see you do it." And he unbound and

let the bear go. Then he sat down on the bench and again began sharpening his knife. And the wolf asked him:

"Daddy, what are you sharpening your knife for?"

"To flay off your skin, that I may make me a warm cap against the winter."

"Oh! Don't flay me, daddy dear, and I'll bring you a whole herd of little sheep."

"Well, see that you do it." And he let the wolf go.

Then he sat down, and began sharpening his knife again. The fox put out her little snout, and asked him:

"Be so kind, dear daddy, and tell me why you are sharpening your knife."

"Little foxes," said the old man, "have nice skins that do capitally for collars and trimmings, and I want to skin you!"

"Oh! Don't take my skin away, daddy dear, and I will bring you hens and geese."

"Very well, see that you do it!" And he let the fox go.

The hare now alone remained, and the old man began sharpening his knife on the hare's account.

"Why do you do that?" asked puss, and he replied:

"Little hares have nice little, soft, warm skins, which will make me nice gloves and mittens against the winter!"

"Oh, daddy dear! Don't flay me, and I'll bring you kale and good cabbage, if only you let me go!"

Then he let the hare go also.

Then they went to bed; but very early in the morning, when it was neither dusk nor dawn, there was a noise in the doorway like "Durrrrrr!"

"Daddy!" cried the old woman, "there's some one scratching at the door; go and see who it is!"

The old man went out, and there was the bear carrying a whole hive full of honey. The old man took the honey from the bear; but no sooner did he lie down than there was another "Durrrrr!" at the door. The old man looked out and saw the wolf driving a whole flock of sheep into the courtyard. Close on his heels came the fox, driving before him geese and hens, and all manner of fowls; and last of all came the hare, bringing cabbage and kale, and all manner of good food. And the old man was glad, and the old woman was glad. And the old man sold the sheep and fowls and got so rich that he needed nothing more. As for the straw-stuffed ox, it stood in the sun till it fell to pieces.

THE STREET MUSICIANS

A DONKEY who had carried sacks to the mill for his master a great many years became so weak that he could not work for a living any longer. His master thought that he would get rid of his old servant, that he might save the cost of his food. The donkey heard of this, and made up his mind to run away. So he took the road to a great city where he had often heard the street band play. "For," thought he, "I can make music as well as they."

He had gone but a little way when he came to a dog stretched out in the middle of the road and panting for breath, as if tired from running.

"Why are you panting so, friend?" asked the donkey.

"Oh, dear!" he replied. "Now that I am old and growing weaker and weaker, and am not able to hunt any more, my master has ordered that I be killed; so I have run away. But how I am to earn a living I am sure I do not know."

"Will you come with me?" said the donkey. "You see, I am going to try my luck as a street musician in the city. I think we might easily earn a living by music. You can play the bass drum and I can play the flute."

"I will go," said the dog, and they both walked on together.

Not long after they saw a cat sitting in the road, with a face as dismal as three days of rainy weather.

"Now what has happened to you, old Whiskers?" said the donkey.

"How can I be happy when I am in fear for my life?" said the cat. "I am getting old, and my teeth are only stumps. I cannot catch mice any longer, and I like to lie behind the stove and purr. But when I found that they were going to drown me, away I ran as fast as my four legs could carry me. But now that I have come away, what am I to do?"

"Go with us to the city," said the donkey. "You often give night concerts, I know, so you can easily become a street musician."

"With all my heart," said the cat, so she walked on with them.

After traveling quite a long distance the three "run-aways" came to a farmyard, and on the gate stood a rooster, crowing with all his might.

"Why are you standing there and making such a fuss?" said the donkey.

"I will tell you," replied the rooster. "I heard the

cook say that there is company coming on Wednesday
and she will want me to put into the soup. That evening
my head will be cut off, so I shall crow at the top of
my voice as long as I can."

"Listen, Red Comb," said the donkey. "Would you
like to run away with us? We are going to the city,
and you will find something better there than to be
made into soup. You have a fine voice, and we are all
musicians."

The rooster was glad to go, and all four went on
together.

They could not reach the city in one day, and evening came on just as they reached a wood, so they
agreed to stay there all night.

The donkey and the dog lay down under a large
tree, the cat stretched herself out on one of the
branches, and the rooster flew to the top, where he
felt quite safe.

Before they slept the rooster, who from his high
roost could see every way, spied far off a tiny light,
and calling to his comrades told them he thought they
were near a house in which a light was shining.

"Then," said the donkey, "we must rouse up and
go on to this light, for no doubt we shall find a good
stopping place there."

The dog said he would be glad of a little piece of

meat, or a couple of bones if he could get nothing more.

Very soon they were on their way to the place where the light shone. It grew larger and brighter as they came nearer to it, till they saw that it came from the window of a small hut. The donkey, who was the tallest, went near and looked in.

"What is to be seen, old Gray Horse?" said the rooster.

"What do I see?" answered the donkey. "Why, a table spread with plenty to eat and drink, and robbers sitting at it and having a good time."

"That ought to be our supper," said the rooster.

"Yes, yes," the donkey answered, "how I wish we were inside."

Then they talked together about how they should drive the robbers away. At last they made a plan that they thought would work. The donkey was to stand on his hind legs and place his forefeet on the windowsill. The dog was to stand on his back. The cat was to stand on the dog's shoulders, and the rooster promised to alight upon the cat's head.

As soon as they were all ready they began to play their music together. The donkey brayed, the dog barked, the cat mewed, the rooster crowed. They made such a noise that the window rattled.

The robbers, hearing the dreadful din, were terribly

frightened, and ran as fast as they could to the woods. The four comrades, rushing in, hurried to the table and ate as if they had had nothing for a month. When they had finished their meal they put out the light, and each one chose a good bed for the night. The don-

key lay down at full length in the yard, the dog crouched behind the door, the cat rolled herself up on the hearth in front of the fire, while the rooster flew to the roof of the hut. They were all so tired after their long journey that they were soon fast asleep.

About midnight one of the robbers, seeing that the

light was out and all quiet, said to his chief: "I do not think that we had any reason to be afraid, after all."

Then he called one of his robbers and sent him to the house to see if it was all right.

The robber, finding everything quiet, went into the kitchen to light a match. Seeing the glaring, fiery eyes of the cat, he thought they were live coals, and held a match toward them that he might light it. But Puss was frightened; she spit at him and scratched his face. This frightened the robber so terribly that he rushed to the door, but the dog, who lay there, sprang out at him and bit him on the leg as he went by.

In the yard he ran against the donkey, who gave him a savage kick, while the rooster on the roof cried out as loud as he could, "Cock-a-doodle-doo."

Then the robber ran back to his chief.

"Oh! oh!" he cried. "In that house is a horrible woman, who flew at me and scratched me down the face with her long fingers. Then by the door stood a man with a knife, who stabbed me in the leg, and out in the yard lay a monster who struck me a hard blow with a huge club; and up on the roof sat the judge, who cried, 'Bring me the scoundrel here.' You may be sure I ran away as fast as I could go."

The robbers never went back to the house, but got

away from that place as quickly as they could. The four musicians liked their new home so well that they thought no more of going on to the city. The last we heard of them, they were still there and having happy times together.

THE TOWN MOUSE AND THE COUNTRY MOUSE

Now you must know that a Town Mouse, once upon a time, went on a visit to his cousin in the country. He was rough and ready, this cousin, but he loved his town friend and made him heartily welcome. Beans and bacon, cheese and bread, were all he had to offer, but he offered them freely.

The Town Mouse rather turned up his long nose at this country fare, and said: "I cannot understand, Cousin, how you can put up with such poor food as this, but of course you cannot expect anything better in the country. Come you with me and I will show you how to live. When you have been in town a week you will wonder how you could ever have stood a country life.

No sooner said than done: the two mice set off for the town and arrived at the Town Mouse's residence late at night.

"You will want some refreshment after our long journey," said the polite Town Mouse, and took his friend into the grand dining-room. There they found

"I cannot understand, Cousin, how you can put up with
such poor food as this."

the remains of a fine feast, and soon the two mice were
eating up jellies and cakes and all that was nice.

Suddenly they heard growling and barking.

"What is that?" said the Country Mouse.

"It is only the dogs of the house," answered the other.

"Only!" said the Country Mouse. "I do not like that
music at my dinner."

Just at that moment the door flew open, in came
two huge mastiffs, and the two mice had to scamper
down and run off.

"Good-by, Cousin," said the Country Mouse.

"What! Going so soon?" said the other.

"Yes," he replied:

*"Better beans and bacon in peace than cakes
and ale in fear."*

THE THREE GOATS

Now you shall hear!

There was once a Boy who had three Goats. All day they leaped and pranced and skipped and climbed up on the rocky hill, but at night the Boy drove them home. One night, when he went to meet them, the frisky things leaped into a turnip field and he could not get them out. Then the Boy sat down on the hillside and cried.

As he sat there a Hare came along. "Why do you cry?" asked the Hare.

"I cry because I can't get the Goats out of the field," answered the Boy.

"*I'll* do it," said the Hare. So he tried, but the Goats would not come. Then the Hare, too, sat down and cried.

Along came a Fox.

"Why do you cry?" asked the Fox.

"I am crying because the Boy cries," said the Hare; "and the Boy is crying because he cannot get the Goats out of the turnip field."

"*I'll* do it," said the Fox.

So the Fox tried, but the Goats would not come. Then the Fox also sat down and cried.

Soon after, a Wolf came along. "Why do you cry?" asked the Wolf.

"I am crying because the Hare cries," said the Fox; "and the Hare cries because the Boy cries; and the Boy cries because he can't get the Goats out of the turnip field."

"*I'll* do it!" said the Wolf. He tried; but the Goats

would not leave the field. So he sat down beside the others and began to cry, too.

After a little, a Bee flew over the hill and saw them all sitting there crying. "Why do you cry?" said the Bee to the Wolf.

"I am crying because the Fox cries; and the Fox cries because the Hare cries; and the Hare cries because the Boy cries; and the Boy cries because he can't get the Goats out of the turnip field."

"*I'll* do it!" said the Bee.

Then the big Animals and the Boy all stopped crying a moment to laugh at the tiny Bee. *He* do it, indeed, when they could not! But the tiny Bee flew away into the turnip field and lit upon one of the Goats and said,

"Buzz-z-z-z!"

And out ran the Goats, every one!

THE WONDERFUL POT

A MAN and his wife were once living in a very small cottage—the smallest and worst-looking hut in the whole village. They were very poor, and often wanted even daily bread. Somehow or other they had managed to keep an only cow, but had been obliged to sell nearly everything else that they had. At length they decided that the cow, too, must go, and the man led her away, intending to bring her to the market. As he walked along the road a stranger approached and hailed him, asking if he intended to sell the animal, and how much he would take for it.

"I think," answered he, "that twenty dollars would be a fair price."

"Money I cannot give you," resumed the stranger, "but I have something which is worth as much as twenty dollars. Here is a pot which I am willing to give for your cow." Saying this, he pulled forth an iron pot with three legs and a handle.

"A pot!" exclaimed the cow's owner. "Of what use would that be to me when I have nothing to put in it?

My wife and children cannot eat an iron pot. No; money is what I need, and what I must have."

The two men stood still a moment looking at each other and at the cow and the pot, when suddenly the three-legged being began to speak. "Just take me," it said. When the poor man heard this he thought that if it could speak no doubt it could do more than that. So he closed the bargain, received the pot, and returned home with it.

When he reached his hut he first went to the stall where the cow had been standing, for he did not dare to appear before his wife at once. Having tied the pot to the manger, he went into the room, asking for something to eat, as he was hungry from his long walk.

"Well," said his wife, "did you make a good bargain at the market? Did you get a good price for the cow?"

"Yes," he said, "the price was fair enough."

"That is well," returned she. "The money will help us a long time."

"No," said he, again, "I received no money for the cow."

"Dear me!" cried she. "What did you receive, then?"

He told her to go and look in the stall.

As soon as the woman learned that the three-legged pot was all that had been paid him for the cow, she scolded and abused him. "You are a great blockhead!"

cried she. "I wish I had myself taken the cow to the market! I never heard of such foolishness!" Thus she went on for a while.

"Clean me and put me on the fire," suddenly shouted the pot.

The woman opened her eyes in great wonder, and now it was her turn to think that if the pot could talk no doubt it could do more than this. She cleaned and washed it carefully and put it on the fire.

"I skip, I skip!" cried the pot.

"How far do you skip?" asked the woman.

"To the rich man's house, to the rich man's house!" it cried again, running from the fireplace to the door, across the yard, and up the road, as fast as the three short legs would carry it.

The rich man lived not very far away. His wife was engaged in baking bread when the pot came running in and jumped up on the table, where it remained standing quite still.

"Ah," exclaimed the woman, "isn't it wonderful! I just needed you for a pudding which must be baked at once." Then she heaped a great many good things into the pot—flour, sugar, butter, raisins, almonds, spices, and so on.

The pot received it all with a good will. At length the pudding was made, but when the rich man's wife reached for it, intending to put it on the stove, tap, tap, tap went the three short legs, and the pot stood on the threshold of the open door.

"Dear me, where are you going with my pudding?" cried the woman.

"To the poor man's home," replied the pot, running down the road at great speed.

When the poor people saw the pot coming back, and found the pudding, they rejoiced, and the man lost no time in asking his wife whether the bargain did not seem to be an excellent one after all. Yes, she was quite pleased and contented.

Next morning the pot again cried: "I skip, I skip!"

"How far do you skip?" asked they.

"To the rich man's barn!" it shouted, running up the road.

When it arrived at the barn it stopped in the door. "Look at that black pot!" cried the men, who were threshing wheat. "Let us see how much it will hold."

"They poured a bushel of wheat into it, but it did not seem to fill rapidly. Another bushel went in, but there was still room. Now every grain of wheat went into the pot, but still it seemed capable of holding much more. As there was no more wheat to be found, the three short legs began to move, and when the men looked around the pot had reached the gate.

"Stop, stop!" called they. "Where do you go with our wheat?"

"To the poor man's home," replied the pot, speeding down the road and leaving the men behind, dismayed and dumfounded.

The poor people were delighted when they received wheat enough to feed them for several years.

On the third morning the pot again skipped up the road. It was a beautiful day. The sun shone so bright and pleasant that the rich man had spread his money on a table near the open window to prevent his gold from becoming moldy. All at once the pot stood on the table before him. He began to count his money over, as wealthy men sometimes like to do, and although he could not imagine where this black pot had come from, he thought it would be a good place to keep his money in the future. So he threw in one handful after another until it held all. At the same moment the pot made a jump from the table to the window sill.

"Wait!" shouted he. "Where do you go with all my money?"

"To the poor man's home," returned the pot, skipping down the road until the money danced within it.

In the middle of the floor in the poor man's hut it stopped, making its owners cry out in rapture over the unexpected treasure. "Clean and wash me," said the pot, "and put me aside."

Next morning it again announced that it was ready to skip.

"How far do you skip?" asked they.

"To the rich man's house!"

So it ran up the road again, never stopping until it had reached the wealthy people's kitchen.

The man happened to be there himself this time, and as soon as he saw it he cried: "There is the pot which carried away our pudding, our wheat, and all our money! I shall make it return what it stole!" He flung himself upon it, but found that he was unable to get off again.

"I skip, I skip!" shouted the pot.

"Skip to the north pole, if you wish!" yelled the man, furiously, trying in vain to free himself.

The three short legs at once moved on, carrying him rapidly down the road. The poor people saw it pass their door; but it never thought of stopping. For all that I know, it went straight to the north pole with its burden.

The poor people became wealthy, and often thought of the wonderful pot with the three short legs which skipped so cheerfully for their good. It was gone, however, and they have never seen it since it carried the rich man toward the north pole.

THE FISHERMAN AND HIS WIFE

THERE was once a fisherman and his wife who lived in a hovel close by the sea, and the fisherman went out every day and fished. And he fished, and fished. So once, as he sat with his line and looked steadily into the clear water, the line sank to the bottom, and as he pulled it up he brought up a great flounder.

Then said the flounder to him: "Hearken, fisherman, to what I tell you. Let me live; I am no real flounder— I am an enchanted Prince. What good would it do you to kill me? I should not taste good. Put me back into the water and let me swim away."

"Now," said the fisherman, "you need not make so many words about it. A flounder that can speak—why, I would just as soon let him go, anyway."

With that he put the fish back into the clear water, and it went to the bottom, leaving a long streak of blood. Then the fisherman got up and went home to his wife in the hovel.

"Well, husband," said his wife, "have you caught nothing?"

"No," said the man. "Yes—that is, I did catch a

flounder; he said he was an enchanted Prince, so I let him swim away."

"Didn't you wish for anything?" asked his wife.

"No," said he. "What should I wish for?"

"Oh, dear!" said the wife. "It is hard indeed always to live in this hovel that is so dirty and small. You should have wished for a little cottage. Go back and tell him we want a little cottage; he will surely give us that."

"Oh," said the man, "why should I go back again?"

"Why," said his wife, "you did catch him and let him swim away again; he surely knows that. Go quickly!"

The man thought it was not right, but he did not like to vex his wife, so he went down to the sea. It was all green and yellow, and no longer so clear. But he stood on the shore and said:

> "O man, O man, if such you be,
> O flounder, flounder in the sea,
> Behold my wife, Dame Ilsabil,
> Would beg a boon against my will."

Up came the fish, and said: "Well, what does she want?"

"Oh," said the man, "I did catch you, and my wife says I really ought to have wished for something. She does not want to live in a hovel any longer; she would like to have a cottage."

"Go," said the flounder. "She has it already."

When the man went home, his wife was no longer in the hovel. There stood in its place a little cottage, and his wife sat before the door on a bench.

She took him by the hand, and said: "Just come in now, husband; see, isn't this much better?"

So they went in, and there was a pretty little parlor and bedroom and a kitchen fitted with whatever could be wished for. Outside was a little yard with hens and ducks, and a little garden full of flowers and fruit.

"See," said the woman. "Isn't this nice?"

"Yes," said the man, "if we always think so. Now we shall live here and be quite content."

"We must think about that," said his wife.

So all went well for a week or two; then the wife said: "Listen, husband—this house is entirely too small, and the garden is very little. The flounder could just as well give us a larger house. I should like to live in a great stone castle. Go ask the flounder for a castle."

"Oh, wife!" said the man. "This cottage is good enough. What do we want with a castle?"

"Nonsense!" said the woman. "Just go to him; the flounder can surely do that."

The man's heart was heavy. "It is not right," he said to himself—and yet he went.

When he came to the sea, the water was quite dark blue, and gray, and thick; it was no longer so green and yellow, but it was quiet.

So he stood there and said:

> "O man, O man, if such you be,
> O flounder, flounder in the sea,
> Behold my wife, Dame Ilsabil,
> Would beg a boon against my will."

"Well, what does she want now?" asked the flounder.

"Alas," said the man, half frightened, "she wants to live in a great stone castle."

"Go to her," said the flounder. "She stands before the door."

Home went the fisherman, and found a great stone castle, and his wife on the steps, just going in. So she took him by the hand. "Come in, husband," she said.

Within was a great hall paved with marble; many servants flung wide the doors; the walls were bright with beautiful tapestries; in the rooms were chairs and tables of pure gold, and crystal chandeliers hung from the ceilings. Outside was a great courtyard with stables for horses and cows. There was also a magnificent garden, and a park with stags and deer and hares and everything that one could wish.

"Now," said the woman, "isn't this beautiful?"

"Ah, yes!" said the man. "Now let it be, and we will live in this beautiful castle, well content."

"We must think about that," said the woman, "and sleep over it."

The next morning the woman woke first; it was just daybreak, and from her bed she saw the beautiful country lying about her. She poked her husband in the side, and said: "Husband, get up and just peep out the window. Look you—couldn't we be King over all that land? Go to the flounder. We will be King."

"Now, wife," said the man, "why should we be King? I don't want to be King."

"Well," said she, "if you won't be King, I will. Go to the flounder I must be King."

So the man went, and he was quite unhappy. "It is not right, it is not right," he kept saying.

But when he came to the sea, it was quite dark gray; the water heaved up from below and had an ill smell. Then he stood by it and said:

> "O man, O man, if such you be,
> O flounder, flounder in the sea,
> Behold my wife, Dame Ilsabil,
> Would beg a boon against my will."

"And what does she want now?" said the flounder.

"Ah, flounder," said the man, "my wife would be King."

"Go to her," said the flounder. "She is King already."

So the man went back, and he found the castle much larger, with a great tower; sentinels stood at the gates, and there were many soldiers with trumpets and kettle-drums. Inside, everything was of marble and gold. In a great court, his wife sat on a high throne of gold and diamonds, with a golden crown on her head, and a scepter of pure gold and jewels in her hand. On both sides stood her pages in a row, each one a head shorter than the next.

Then he stood before her, and said: "Well, wife, are you King?"

"Yes," said she, "I am King."

So after he had stood and looked at her for a long time, he said, "Wife, now that you are King, let all else be; now we will wish for nothing more."

"Nay, husband," cried she, quite uneasily, "time passes heavily. I can bear it no longer. Go to the flounder. I am King—now I must be Emperor."

"Alas," cried the man, "the flounder can't make you Emperor! I can't say that to the fish; there is but one Emperor in the land."

"What?" cried the woman. "I am King; you are only my husband. Will you go at once?"

So the man had to go. As he went, however, he was troubled, and he kept muttering to himself: "It won't end well, it won't end well. 'Emperor' is too shameful; the flounder will at last be worn out."

With that he came to the sea, and it was quite black and thick; the wind blew, and white foam arose. The man was frightened, but he stood and cried:

> "O man, O man, if such you be,
> O flounder, flounder in the sea,
> Behold my wife, Dame Ilsabil,
> Would beg a boon against my will."

"What now?" asked the flounder.

"Ah, flounder," said he, "my wife would be Emperor."

"Go to her," said the flounder. "She is Emperor already."

So when the man came to the castle, it was much larger, with a great tower of polished marble with figures of gold and alabaster. Inside were barons and counts and dukes. Doors of pure gold were thrown open, and there sat his wife on a throne of one piece of gold two miles high; she wore a great golden crown with diamonds and carbuncles; in one hand she held a scepter, and in the other a globe. On both sides stood her pages, arranged according to size, from the tallest giant down to the smallest dwarf, not so large as a man's little finger.

The man stood before her, and said, "So, wife, now you are Emperor?"

"Yes," said she, "now I am Emperor."

After he had looked at her for some time, he said, "Well, wife, now that you are Emperor, wish for nothing more."

"Husband," said she, "why do you stand there? Now I am Emperor, but I will also be Pope. Go to the flounder."

"Alas, wife," cried the man, "what do you not want! You can't be Pope: there is but one Pope in Christendom. The fish can't make you Pope."

"Man," said she, "what nonsense! If he can make me Emperor, he can make me Pope. So go to him at once: I am Emperor, you are only my husband. Will you go?"

He was afraid, and went, but he shivered and shook. A high wind blew over the land and the leaves fell from the trees; the water arose and roared as if it were boiling; in the distance ships were firing guns in their distress, pitching and tossing on the waves. And yet there was still a bit of blue in the midst of the sky, although on every side it was red as in a storm.

Then, very anxious, he stood and said:

> "O man, O man, if such you be,
> O flounder, flounder in the sea,
> Behold my wife, Dame Ilsabil,
> Would beg a boon against my will."

"Well, what now?" asked the flounder.

"Alas," said the man, "she will be Pope."

"Go to her," said the flounder. "She is now Pope."

So he went home, and found what seemed to be a great church surrounded with palaces. He pushed his way through the crowd. Inside, everything was lighted with thousands and thousands of candles. His wife, clad in pure gold, was sitting on a very lofty throne with three great golden crowns on her head. Round about her was much churchly splendor; on both sides of her were rows of candles of all sizes, from the highest tower down to the very smallest rushlight. All the emperors and kings were on their knees before her, kissing her shoe.

"Wife," said the man, after he had looked at her for a long time, as if dazed, "are you now Pope?"

"Yes," said she, "I am Pope."

Then he said, "Well, wife, if you are Pope, do let well enough alone!"

"Wife, are you now Pope?"

But she looked as stiff as a post, and did not move.

Then he said, "Wife, be contented now you are Pope; you can become nothing greater."

"I'll think about that," said the woman.

That night the man slept right well and soundly, for he had run about a good deal, but the woman could not sleep; she tossed about trying to think what she should be now. At last the sun began to rise, and when the woman saw the red of dawn, she sat up in bed and looked at it, and when she saw the sun coming up, she said: "Why, that is it! Why can't I order the sun and moon to rise? Husband," she cried, poking him with her elbow, "wake up! Go to the flounder. I will be Lord of the sun and moon."

The man was still almost asleep, but he was so horrified that he fell out of bed. He thought that he must have heard wrong, and he rubbed his eyes and said, "Oh, wife, wh-what did you say?"

"Husband," said she, "if I can't order the sun and moon to rise, and must look on and see them rising, I can't bear it. I shan't have another peaceful hour." Then she looked at him so terribly that a shudder ran over him.

"Go at once!" she cried. "I will rule the sun and moon."

"Alas, wife," cried the man, and fell upon his knees

before her, "I beg you, go on as you are and be Pope!"

Then she fell into a rage, and cried, "I will not bear this any longer. Will you go?"

So he dressed and ran away like a madman.

A great storm was raging; houses and trees toppled over; mountains trembled and rocks rolled into the sea. Then the sea came in with black, white-crested waves as high as mountains.

The fisherman cried—but he could not hear his own words:

> "O man, O man, if such you be,
> O flounder, flounder in the sea,
> Behold my wife, Dame Ilsabil,
> Would beg a boon against my will."

"And what does she want now?" asked the flounder.

"Ah!" said the man. "She will command the sun and moon.

"Go to her," said the flounder, "and you will find her back again in the hovel."

And there they are living to this very day.

THE FLYING SHIP

ONCE upon a time there was a rich Czar. He had everything he could wish for.

One day he said, "If I could fly like the birds, I should be happy."

So he called his wise men and said, "Make me a ship that will fly like a bird."

But the wise men answered, "We do not know how to make a flying ship."

So the Czar sent word all over the land, "The man who brings me a flying ship shall have my daughter and half of my kingdom."

Now, near the palace lived an old man and an old woman who had three sons.

The eldest son said, "I will go and find a ship that can fly; then I can have the Czar's daughter and half of the kingdom." So he set off with his mother's blessing.

Then the next son said, "I shall try too," and off he set.

The two brothers went a long, long way, but they found no flying ship.

Then Ivan, the youngest son, said, "I must find the flying ship."

"No, my son," said his mother, "you are too young to go."

But Ivan kept saying, "I must go! I must go!" So his mother gave him her blessing and he set off.

He went a long way, and at last he met an old man. "Where are you going, my lad?" said the old man.

"I am going to get a flying ship for the Czar," replied Ivan.

"And can you make a flying ship?" asked the old man.

"No, I can not make one, but they will make one for me somewhere," answered Ivan.

"And where is that somewhere?" asked the old man.

"I do not know," said the lad.

"Well, then," said the old man, "let us sit down and eat. What have you in your knapsack?"

"There is only dry bread in it," said Ivan. "I am ashamed to show you."

"Your mother has given it to you. Do not be ashamed of it," said the old man. "Let us see what you have."

So Ivan opened his knapsack. What did he see? There lay white rolls and many kinds of meat.

"Here is a fine feast," said the old man. And they sat down on the grass and ate.

"Now," said the old man, "go into the woods. Bow three times to the first oak tree you see, and strike it with your ax. Then fall to the earth with your face down. Wait there until you hear a whirring sound. Then look up and you will see a flying ship. Get into it and fly where you like. Be kind to all you meet and take them into the ship with you."

"Thank you," said Ivan, and he went into the woods. He did just as the old man told him to do. He bowed three times before the first oak tree and struck it with his ax. Then he fell with his face to the ground. In a little while he heard a whirring sound. He looked up and there was the flying ship.

Ivan got into the ship and away it flew. And look! He saw a man lying with his ear to the ground.

"Good day, Uncle," said Ivan. "What are you doing?"

"I can hear all around the world," said the man. "My name is Sharp Ear."

"Come and ride with me," said Ivan.

"Thank you," said the man, and he climbed into the ship. Away they flew. They flew and flew. And look! There was a man hopping on one foot. The other foot was tied to his ear.

"Good day, Uncle," said Ivan. "Why do you hop on one foot?"

"Oh," said the man, "if I untie my foot I can step halfway around the world. My name is Swift Foot."

"Come and ride with us," said Ivan.

"Thank you," said Swift Foot, and he climbed into the ship. Away they flew. They flew and flew. And look! They saw a man with a gun.

"Good day, Uncle," said Ivan, "what are you shooting at? There is not a bird in sight."

"Oh," said the man, "I can hit a bird one hundred miles away. My name is Sure Shot."

"Come and ride with us," said Ivan.

"Thank you," said the man, and he climbed into the ship. Away they flew. They flew and flew. And look! There was a man with a sack of bread on his back.

"Good day, Uncle," said Ivan. "Where are you going?"

"I am going to get some bread for my dinner," answered the man.

"But you have a big sack of bread on your back," said Ivan.

"Oh, that is only a mouthful," answered the man. "They call me Gobbler."

"Come and ride with us," said Ivan.

"Thank you," said the man, and he climbed into

the ship. Away they flew. They flew and flew. And look! There was a man walking by a lake.

"Good day, Uncle, what are you looking for?" said Ivan.

"I want a drink," answered the man. "I am thirsty."

"There is a whole lake of water," said the lad, "why don't you drink of that?"

"That would not make a mouthful for me," said the man. "They call me Drinker."

"Come and ride with us," said Ivan.

"Thank you," said the man, and he climbed into the ship. And away they flew. They flew and flew. And look! There was a man with a great bundle of straw on his back.

"Good day to you," said Ivan. "Where are you going with that straw?"

"I am going to the village," answered the man.

"Have they no straw in the village?" asked Ivan.

"They have no straw like this; this is magic straw," answered the man. "When it is hot I lay this straw down and it becomes cool."

"Come and ride with us," said Ivan.

"Thank you," said the man, and he climbed into the ship. Away they flew. They flew and flew. And look! There was a man with a bundle of wood on his back.

"Good day, Uncle," said Ivan, "why do you drag that bundle of wood about?"

"This is magic wood," said the man. "If I put it on the ground a great army will spring up."

"Come and ride with us," said Ivan.

"Thank you," said the man. And he climbed into the ship. And away they flew. They flew and flew. And look! There was the Czar's castle.

The people in the castle heard the whirring sound. They ran out to see what it was. "Look," they cried, "there is the flying ship!"

The Czar looked out of the window and saw the ship. "Some great prince has won my daughter," he said. So he sent out a servant to welcome him.

Soon the servant came back. "O Czar," said he, "there is only a poor peasant lad in the ship."

The Czar was very angry. "My daughter can not marry a peasant. But I must have the flying ship. I must give him some hard tasks to do." So he said to his servant, "Go tell this peasant lad that he must bring me some living and singing water from the end of the world. And he must bring it before my dinner is over."

Now Sharp Ear heard the Czar's command, and he told Ivan.

"What shall I do?" asked Ivan. "It would take me a year to go to the end of the world."

There was the Czar's castle.

"Do not be afraid," said Swift Foot. "I will get some living and singing water for you. Untie my foot and I will step to the end of the world for it. That will be easy for me."

Just then the servant came out and gave Ivan the Czar's order. "Tell the Czar that he shall be obeyed," said Ivan.

Swift Foot was off in a minute and found the living and singing water. "I have time enough," he said. "I will rest by this old mill." So he sat down and fell asleep.

The King's dinner was almost ended, and Swift Foot had not returned. Sharp Ear put his ear to the ground. "I can hear Swift Foot snoring by the old mill," said he.

"Then I will wake him," said Sure Shot.

And he took his gun and shot into the mill. Swift Foot awoke and was at the Czar's castle in a minute.

The Czar took the water, but he was very angry. So he said to his servant, "Go tell the lad that he must eat twenty roasted oxen and twenty tons of bread at one meal."

Again Sharp Ear heard the Czar's order and told Ivan.

"What shall I do?" asked Ivan. "It would take me twenty years to eat twenty oxen and twenty tons of bread."

"Do not be afraid," said Gobbler. "Twenty oxen and twenty tons of bread will only make one meal for me. I will eat it."

Just then the servant came out and gave Ivan the Czar's order.

"Tell the Czar that he shall be obeyed," said Ivan.

The twenty roasted oxen and twenty tons of bread were brought to the ship and Gobbler ate it all up.

"I am still hungry," he said. "They might have given me more."

The Czar was more angry than ever. So he ordered Ivan to drink forty barrels of water. A barrel held forty pails of water.

Again Sharp Ear heard the Czar's command and told Ivan.

"What shall I do?" asked Ivan. "I could not drink one pail of water."

"Do not be afraid," said Drinker. "I can drink the forty barrels at once."

The forty barrels of water were sent to the ship. Soon it was all gone. "I am still thirsty," said Drinker.

The Czar said, "We must trick this lad." So he ordered Ivan to get ready for the wedding. "Make the iron bathroom red-hot," said the Czar to his servant.

Sharp Ear heard the order and told Ivan.

"What shall I do?" said Ivan. "No one can save me now."

"Do not be afraid," said the man with the straw. "Take me with you."

Ivan went into the bathroom and the man with the straw went with him. "I must put straw on the floor," said the man.

Now the magic straw made the bathroom cool, so Ivan lay down by the stove.

In the morning the servant opened the door. He found Ivan lying by the stove singing.

When the Czar heard this he said: "What can I do? I must get rid of this peasant. He must not marry my daughter, but I must have his flying ship. I will order him to raise a large army. He can not do that."

Again Sharp Ear heard the Czar's command and told Ivan.

"Now I am lost," said Ivan, sadly. "You can not help me this time."

"You have forgotten me," said the man with the bundle of wood. "I will place my magic sticks around the castle, and soon you will see a great army."

The servant came and told Ivan the Czar's command.

"The Czar shall be obeyed," said Ivan. "But I must have his daughter, or my army shall break down the castle."

The Czar laughed when he heard that Ivan would break down his castle.

That night the magic wood was placed around the castle. Each piece of wood became a soldier. There stood a great army of men. Bugles sounded, drums began to beat, and the soldiers began to march.

The Czar awoke, and he looked out of the window. The soldiers presented arms.

The Czar was filled with terror. "I can do nothing against such a great army. This peasant shall have my daughter."

So he sent his royal robes and jewels to Ivan, and invited him to the castle.

Ivan put on the royal robes and jewels. He looked so handsome that the princess fell in love with him.

There was a grand wedding and a great banquet. For once Gobbler and Drinker had all they wanted to eat and drink. The Czar gave Ivan half of the kingdom, and they were all happy ever after.

CINDERELLA

ONCE upon a time there lived a girl who was as kind and gentle as she was beautiful.

As she had no home of her own, she worked for a woman who had two proud and haughty daughters.

Cinderella, the maid was called, because after her work was finished she sat by the fireplace in the kitchen raking the cinders; she washed all the dishes and scrubbed the floors, and took care of the rooms of the two sisters. Their beds were made of softest down. In their rooms were mirrors that reached from the floor to the ceiling, before which they admired themselves for hours at a time. Poor Cinderella slept on a bundle of straw in the garret and had only rags to dress in.

The two sisters were unkind to Cinderella, but no matter how harshly she was treated she was always sweet and good-tempered.

One day the King's son sent out invitations to a grand ball. The sisters were very happy indeed because they were invited to attend.

For days and days they talked of nothing but how they would dress and how beautiful they would look.

"I shall wear my red velvet gown trimmed with my fine point lace," said the elder sister.

The other sister said she would look far more beautiful in her gown of blue silk covered with gold brocade and studded with diamonds.

They quarreled so about their clothes that Cinderella tried to make peace between them. She offered to help them dress for the ball and promised to arrange their hair. The sisters were very willing to accept her help because Cinderella had perfect taste. All this planning made extra work for Cinderella. She ironed their ruffles and fluted their frills, but never a word of praise or thanks did she receive for her efforts.

The evening of the ball as Cinderella was arranging the elder sister's hair, the sister said to her, "Cinderella, how would you like to go to the ball?"

"Oh," said Cinderella, "I would love to, but how could I go? I have nothing to wear."

"Of course," replied the sister, "you could not go. How the guests would laugh to see a cinder-maid at the ball!"

After the sisters had gone Cinderella went into the kitchen and sat before the fire crying silently.

Suddenly, her fairy godmother appeared and, seeing that she was weeping, said: "What is the matter, my child? Why are you crying?"

"Oh," sobbed Cinderella, "I wish—I wish—"

"I know what you wish," said her fairy godmother. "You wish you could go to the ball, and so you shall. Now, dry your eyes and run into the garden and bring me a pumpkin."

Cinderella did as she was told and came running back with the largest pumpkin she could find.

The fairy godmother touched it with her wand and turned it into a beautiful golden coach. "Now for some horses," said her fairy godmother. "Bring me the mouse trap from the pantry." In the mouse trap were six little gray mice. The fairy godmother opened the trap, and as each mouse ran out she touched it with her wand and it became a beautiful dapple-gray horse.

"But what are we to do for a coachman?"

Cinderella thought she could find a rat in the rat trap. "That is a splendid idea, my dear," said the fairy godmother. Off Cinderella ran, bringing back a trap in which were three large rats. The fairy godmother chose the largest and, touching it with her wand, turned it into a splendid coachman dressed in a suit of green trimmed with gold buttons.

They now needed footmen. The fairy godmother told Cinderella that she would find six lizards in the garden behind the watering pot. These she touched with her wand, and six footmen with green suits trimmed with gold lace jumped up on the coach as if they had been doing this all their lives.

The fairy godmother then touched Cinderella with her wand. The ragged dress was changed into a gown of gold and silver cloth studded with pearls and other precious stones. On her feet were a pair of beautiful crystal slippers, the smallest in the world.

"Cinderella," said her fairy godmother, "you may now go to the ball. But remember, you are to leave before twelve o'clock or your coach will turn into a pumpkin, your horses into mice, your footmen into lizards, and your beautiful clothes back into rags."

Cinderella gayly promised to do as she was told and, stepping into her golden coach, was quickly driven away.

When she reached the courtyard of the King's palace, word was sent to the Prince that a beautiful and unknown Princess had arrived.

The Prince came out to meet her and led her into the ballroom. As they entered the room, the musicians stopped playing, the guests stopped dancing, and everyone stood and wondered who the beautiful Princess could be. Even the King remarked to the Queen that he had never seen any one quite so lovely in many years. The ladies of the court greatly admired her clothes and wondered just where they could find some one who could make just such a gown for them.

The Prince led her to the place of honor and then danced with her the entire evening.

At eleven o'clock a splendid supper was served. Cinderella seated herself beside the sisters and spoke pleasantly to them. She also shared with them some of the fruit that the Prince had given to her.

The two sisters were very proud indeed to have the beautiful Princess, whom the Prince had so highly honored, pay this marked attention to them. They did not, of course, recognize the little cinder-maid.

When the clock struck quarter to twelve, Cinderella arose and curtsied to the King and Queen. They invited her to attend another ball that was to be given the next evening. Then the Prince led her to her coach and stood looking after her as she was driven away.

Her fairy godmother was waiting for her when she reached home. Cinderella was overjoyed with everything that had happened. While she was telling her godmother about the ball, the sisters knocked at the door. Cinderella, rubbing her eyes as if she had been asleep for some time, opened the door.

"How late you are!" she said.

"Oh," replied the elder sister, "if you had been to

the ball and had seen the beautiful Princess we saw, you would not think it late."

"Who was she?" asked Cinderella.

"No one knew," said the younger sister, "not even the Prince. She was very lovely to us. She sat beside us at the supper and gave us some of the fruit the Prince had given her."

"How I would love to go to the ball to-morrow night, just to see this Princess!" said Cinderella. "Oh, my Lady Javotte"—for that was the name of the elder sister—"will you please loan me your yellow dress which you wear every day, that I may go?"

At this Lady Javotte laughed and said that she would never think of loaning her dress to a cinder-maid. Cinderella was very glad indeed to hear this because she really would not have known what to do if Lady Javotte had been willing to loan her the dress.

The next evening, after the sisters had gone to the ball, the fairy godmother appeared. Touching Cinderella again with her wand, she made her even more beautiful than the night before. As Cinderella drove away, the fairy godmother warned her to leave the ball before midnight.

The Prince was waiting for her when she reached the Palace. He led her once more to the place of honor and never left her all during the evening.

Cinderella enjoyed herself so much that the time slipped by unnoticed. Just as supper was being served the clock began to strike the hour of twelve. She suddenly remembered the fairy's warning. Rising to her feet she ran swiftly out of the Palace. In her haste, she dropped one of her crystal slippers on the steps.

The Prince, who was following her, quickly picked it up and slipped it into his pocket. Looking up, he saw that the Princess had disappeared.

When Cinderella reached home all she had left of her lovely clothes was one little crystal slipper; the Prince had the mate to it.

The Prince asked the guards if they had seen the Princess, but they had seen only a little beggar maiden, dressed in rags, slipping through the Palace Gates.

Cinderella waited for the sisters to come home, and asked them if the Princess had been at the ball.

"Yes," said they, "and she was even more beautiful than the evening before. But suddenly, at twelve o'clock, she disappeared, and no one knew where she had gone." They told her, however, that the Prince had found one of her crystal slippers. She had dropped it in her flight and they were certain that he would find her, no matter where she was hidden.

The Prince asked every one for information about the Princess, but no one was able to help him.

At last he sent out messengers with trumpets announcing to all that he would marry whomever the slipper would fit. This caused great excitement in the kingdom. Every lady hoped that the crystal slipper would fit her.

First the slipper was tried on all the princesses, then on all the duchesses, then on all the grand ladies, and at last it came to the home of the two sisters. Each, of course, tried to force her foot into it, but the little slipper would not fit either of them.

Cinderella, who was standing watching, at last asked, timidly, "May I try?"

At this the sisters laughed and cried: "What! A cinder-maid try on the crystal slipper?"

The messenger looked at Cinderella and thought her very fair indeed, and replied, "The Prince said that every maiden in the kingdom, could, if she wished, try on the slipper."

Cinderella then seated herself on a stool. The messenger knelt before her and put the slipper on her foot. It fitted her as if it had been made for her, and so it had. Then, to the great amazement of the sisters, Cinderella drew the other slipper out of her pocket and slipped it on her foot.

At that moment her fairy godmother appeared. Touching Cinderella with her wand, she changed her once more into the beautiful Princess.

When the sisters saw that Cinderella was the lovely lady of the ball, they knelt before her, begging her forgiveness. She put her arms around them, raised them to their feet, and told them that she forgave them freely.

The messenger then led Cinderella to the Palace, where the Prince was waiting for her. In a few days they were married in royal state and lived happily ever after.

THE PRINCESS ON THE GLASS HILL

ONCE upon a time there was a man who had a meadow which lay on the side of a mountain, and in the meadow there was a barn in which he stored hay. But there had not been much hay in the barn for the last two years, for every St. John's night, when the grass was in the height of its vigor, it was all eaten clean up, just as if a whole flock of sheep had gnawed it down to the ground during the night. This happened once, and it happened twice, but then the man got tired of losing his crop, and said to his sons—he had three of them, and the third was called Cinderlad—that one of them must go and sleep in the barn on St. John's night, for it was absurd to let the grass be eaten up again, blade and stalk, as it had been the last two years, and the one who went to watch must keep a sharp lookout, the man said.

The eldest was quite willing to go to the meadow; he would watch the grass, he said, and he would do it so well that neither man, nor beast, nor even the devil himself should have any of it. So when evening came he went to the barn, and lay down to sleep, but when night was drawing near there was such a rumbling and such an earthquake that the walls and roof shook again, and the lad jumped up and took to his heels as fast as he could, and never even looked back, and the barn remained empty that year just as it had been for the last two.

Next St. John's night the man again said that he could not go on in this way, losing all the grass in the outlying field year after year, and that one of his sons must just go there and watch it, and watch well too. So the next oldest son was willing to show what he could do. He went to the barn and lay down to sleep, as his brother had done; but when night was drawing near there was a great rumbling, and then an earthquake, which was even worse than that on the former St. John's night, and when the youth heard it he was terrified, and went off, running as if for a wager.

The year after it, was Cinderlad's turn, but when he made ready to go the others laughed at him, and mocked him. "Well, you are just the right one to watch the hay, you who have never learned anything but how to sit among the ashes and bake yourself!" said they. Cinderlad, however, did not trouble himself about what they said, but when evening drew near rambled away to the outlying field. When he got there he went into the barn and lay down, but in about an hour's time the rumbling and creaking began, and it was frightful to hear it. "Well, if it gets no worse than that, I can manage to stand it," thought Cinderlad. In a little time the creaking began again, and the earth quaked so that all the hay flew about the boy. "Oh! if it gets no worse than that I can manage to stand it," thought Cinderlad. But then came a third rumbling, and a third earthquake, so violent that the boy thought the walls and roof had fallen down, but when that was over everything suddenly grew as still as death around him. "I am pretty sure that it will come again," thought Cinderlad; but no, it did not. Everything was quiet, and everything stayed quiet, and when he had lain still a short time he heard something that sounded as if a horse were standing chewing just outside the barn door. He stole away to the door, which was ajar, to see what was there, and a horse was standing eating. It was so big, and fat, and fine a horse that Cinderlad had never seen one like it before, and a saddle and bridle lay upon it, and a complete suit of armor for a knight, and everything was of copper, and so bright that it shone again. "Ha, ha! it is thou who eatest up our hay then," thought the boy. "But I will stop that." So he made haste, and took out his steel for striking fire, and threw it over the horse, and then it had no power to stir from the spot, and became so tame that the boy could do what he liked with it. So he mounted it and rode away to a place which no one knew of but himself, and there he tied it up. When he went home again his brothers laughed and asked how he had got on.

"You didn't lie long in the barn, if even you have been so far as the field!" said they.

"I lay in the barn till the sun rose, but I saw nothing and heard nothing, not I," said the boy. "God knows what there was to make you two so frightened."

"Well, we shall soon see whether you have watched the meadow or not," answered the brothers, but when they got there the grass was all standing just as long and as thick as it had been the night before.

The next St. John's night it was the same thing once again: neither of the two brothers dared to go to the outlying field to watch the crop, but Cinderlad went, and everything happened exactly the same as on the previous St. John's night, first there was a rumbling and an earthquake, and then there was another, and then a third; but all three earthquakes were much, very much more violent than they had been the year before. Then everything became still as death again, and the boy heard something chewing outside the barn door, so he stole as softly as he could to the door, which was slightly ajar, and again there was a horse standing close by the wall of the house, eating and chewing, and it was far larger and fatter than the first horse, and it had a saddle on its back, and a bridle was on it too, and a full suit of armor for a knight, all of bright silver, and as beautiful as any one could wish to see. "Ho, ho!" thought the boy. "Is it thou who eatest up our hay in the night? but I will put a stop to that." So he took out his steel for striking fire, and threw it over the horse's mane, and the beast stood there as quiet as a lamb. Then the boy rode this horse, too, away to the place where he kept the other, and then went home again.

"I suppose you will tell us that you have watched well again this time," said the brothers.

"Well, so I have," said Cinderlad. So they went there again, and there the grass was, standing as high and as thick as it had been before, but that did not make them any kinder to Cinderlad.

When the third St. John's night came neither of the two elder brothers dared to lie in the outlying barn to watch the grass, for they had been so heartily frightened the nights that they had slept there that they could not get over it; but Cinderlad dared to go, and everything happened just the same as on the two former nights. There were three earthquakes, each worse than the other, and the last flung the boy from one wall of the barn to the other, but then everything suddenly became still as death. When he had lain quietly a short time, he heard something chewing outside the barn door; then he once more stole to the door, which was slightly ajar, and behold, a horse was standing just outside it, which was much larger and fatter than the two others he had caught. "Ho, ho! It is thou, then, who art eating up our hay this time," thought the boy. "But I will put a stop to that." So he pulled out his steel for striking fire, and threw it over the horse, and it stood as still as if it had been nailed to the field, and the boy could do just what he liked with it. Then he mounted it and rode away to the place where he had the two others, and then he went home again. Then the two brothers mocked him just as they had done before, and told him that they could see that he must have watched the grass very carefully that night, for he looked just as if he were walking in his sleep; but Cinderlad did not trouble himself about that, but just bade them go to the field and see. They did go, and this time too the grass was standing, looking as fine and as thick as ever.

The King of the country in which Cinderlad's father dwelt had a daughter whom he would give to no one who could not ride up to the top of the glass hill, for there was a high, high hill of glass, slippery as ice, and it was close to the King's palace. Upon the very top of this the King's daughter was to sit with three gold apples in her lap, and the man who could ride up and take the three golden apples should marry her, and have half the kingdom. The King had this proclaimed in every church in the whole kingdom, and in many other kingdoms too. The Princess was very beautiful, and all who saw her fell violently in love with her, even in spite of themselves. So it is needless to say that all the princes and knights were eager to win her, and half the kingdom besides, and that for this cause they came riding thither from the very end of the world, dressed so splendidly that their raiments gleamed in the sunshine, and riding on horses which seemed to dance as they went, and there was not one of these princes who did not think that he was sure to win the Princess.

When the day appointed by the King had come, there was such a host of knights and princes under the glass hill that they seemed to swarm, and every one who could walk or even creep was there too, to see who would win the King's daughter. Cinderlad's two brothers were there too, but they would not hear of letting him go with them, for he was so dirty and black with sleeping and grubbing among the ashes that they said every one would laugh at them if they were seen in the company of such an oaf.

"Well, then, I will go by myself," said Cinderlad.

When the two brothers got to the glass hill, all the princes and knights were trying to ride up it, and their horses were in a foam; but it was all in vain, for no sooner did the horses set foot upon the hill than down they slipped, and there was not one which could get even so much as a couple of yards up. Nor was that strange, for the hill was as smooth as glass window-pane, and as steep as the side of a house. But they were all eager to win the King's daughter and half the kingdom, so they rode and they slipped, and thus it went on. At length all the horses were so tired that they could do no more, and so hot that the foam dropped from them and the riders were forced to give up the attempt. The King was just thinking that he would cause it to be proclaimed that the riding should begin afresh on the following day, when perhaps it might go better, when suddenly a knight came riding up on so fine a horse that no one had ever seen the like of it before, and the knight had armor of copper, and his bridle was of copper too, and all his accouterments were so bright that they shone again. The other knights all called out to him that he might just as well spare himself the trouble of trying to ride up the glass hill, for it was of no use to try; but he did not heed them, and rode straight off to it, and went up as if it were nothing at all. Thus he rode for a long way—it may have been a third part of the way up—but when he had got so far he turned his horse round and rode down again. But the Princess thought that she had never yet seen so handsome a knight, and while he was riding up she was sitting thinking: "Oh! how I hope he may be able to come up to the top!" And when she saw that he was turning his horse back she threw one of the golden apples down after him, and it rolled into his shoe. But when he had come down from off the hill he rode away, and that so fast that no one knew what had become of him.

So all the princes and knights were bidden to present themselves before the King that night, so that he who had ridden so far up the glass hill might show the golden apple which the King's daughter had thrown down. But no one had anything to show. One knight presented himself after another, and none could show the apple.

At night, too, Cinderlad's brothers came home again and had a long story to tell about the riding up the glass hill. At first, they said, there was not one who was able to get even so much as one step up, but then came a knight who had armor of copper, and a bridle of

copper, and his armor and trappings were so bright
that they shone to a great distance, and it was something like a sight to see him riding. He rode one-third
of the way up the glass hill, and he could easily have
ridden the whole of it if he had liked; but he had
turned back, for he had made up his mind that that
was enough for once. "Oh! I should have liked to see
him too, that I should," said Cinderlad, who was as
usual sitting by the chimney among the cinders. "You
indeed!" said the brothers. "You look as if you were
fit to be among such great lords, nasty beast that you
are to sit there!"

Next day the brothers were for setting out again,
and this time too Cinderlad begged them to let him go
with them and see who rode; but no, they said he was
not fit to do that, for he was much too ugly and dirty.
"Well, well, then I will go all alone by myself," said
Cinderlad. So the brothers went to the glass hill, and
all the princes and knights began to ride again, and
this time they had taken care to rough the shoes of
their horses; but that did not help them: they rode and
they slipped as they had done the day before, and not
one of them could even get so far as a yard up the hill.
When they had tired out their horses, so that they
could do no more, they again had to stop altogether.
But just as the King was thinking that it would be well

to proclaim that the riding should take place next day for the last time, so that they might have one more chance, he suddenly bethought himself that it would be well to wait a little longer to see if the knight in copper armor would come on this day too. But nothing was to be seen of him. Just as they were still looking for him, however, came a knight riding on a steed that was much, much finer than that which the knight in copper armor had ridden, and this knight had silver armor and a silver saddle and bridle, and all were so bright that they shone and glistened when he was a long way off. Again the other knights called to him, and said that he might just as well give up the attempt to ride up the glass hill, for it was useless to try; but the knight paid no heed to that, but rode straight away to the glass hill, and went still farther up than the knight in copper armor had gone; but when he had ridden two-thirds of the way up he turned his horse round, and rode down again. The Princess liked this knight still better than she had liked the other, and sat longing that he might be able to get up above, and when she saw him turning back she threw the second apple after him, and it rolled into his shoe, and as soon as he had got down the glass hill he rode away so fast that no one could see what had become of him.

In the evening, when every one was to appear before

the King and Princess, in order that he who had the golden apple might show it, one knight went in after another, but none of them had a golden apple to show.

At night the two brothers went home as they had done the night before, and told how things had gone, and how every one had ridden, but no one had been able to get up the hill. "But last of all," they said, "came one in silver armor, and he had a silver bridle on his horse, and a silver saddle, and oh, but he could ride! He took his horse two-thirds of the way up the hill, but then he turned back. He was a fine fellow," said the brothers, "and the Princess threw the second golden apple to him!"

"Oh, how I should have liked to see him too!" said Cinderlad.

"Oh, indeed! He was a little brighter than the ashes that you sit grubbing among, you dirty black creature!" said the brothers.

On the third day everything went just as on the former days. Cinderlad wanted to go with them to look at the riding, but the two brothers would not have him in their company, and when they got to the glass hill there was no one who could ride even so far as a yard up it, and every one waited for the knight in silver armor, but he was neither to be seen nor heard of. At last, after a long time, came a knight riding upon a horse that was such a fine one, its equal had never yet been seen. The knight had golden armor, and the horse a golden saddle and bridle, and these were all so bright that they shone and dazzled every one, even while the knight was still at a great distance. The other princes and knights were not able even to call to tell him how useless it was to try to ascend the hill, so amazed were they at the sight of his magnificence. He rode straight away to the glass hill, and galloped up it as if it were no hill at all, so that the Princess had not even time to wish that he might get up the whole way. As soon as he had ridden to the top, he took the third golden apple from the lap of the Princess, and then turned his horse about and rode down again, and vanished from their sight before any one was able to say a word to him.

When the two brothers came home again at night, they had much to tell of how the riding had gone off that day, and at last they told about the knight in the golden armor too. "He was a fine fellow, he was! Such another splendid knight is not to be found on earth!" said the brothers.

"Oh, how I should have liked to see him too!" said Cinderlad.

"Well, he shone nearly as brightly as the coal heaps

He rode straight away to the glass hill.

that thou art always lying raking amongst, dirty black creature that thou art!" said the brothers.

Next day all the knights and princes were to appear before the King and the Princess—it had been too late for them to do it the night before—in order that he who had the golden apple might produce it. They all went in turn, first princes, and then knights, but none of them had a golden apple.

"But somebody must have it," said the King, "for with our own eyes we all saw a man ride up and take it." So he commanded that every one in the kingdom should come to the palace, and see if he could show the apple. And one after another they all came, but no one had the golden apple, and after a long, long time Cinderlad's two brothers came likewise. They were the last of all, so the King inquired of them if there was no one else in the kingdom left to come.

"Oh! yes, we have a brother," said the two, "but he never got the golden apple! He never left the cinder heap on any of the three days."

"Never mind that," said the King. "As every one else has come to the palace, let him come too."

So Cinderlad was forced to go to the King's palace.

"Hast thou the golden apple?" asked the King.

"Yes, here is the first, and here is the second, and here is the third, too," said Cinderlad, and he took all three apples out of his pocket, and with that threw off his sooty rags, and appeared there before them in his bright golden armor, which gleamed as he stood.

"Thou shalt have my daughter, and the half of my kingdom, and thou hast well earned both!" said the King. So there was a wedding, and Cinderlad got the King's daughter, and every one made merry at the wedding, for all of them could make merry, though they could not ride up the glass hill, and if they have not left off their merry-making they must be at it still.

THE SLEEPING BEAUTY

LONG, long ago there lived a king and a queen, who owned wide forests, great gardens, and beautiful palaces. Still they were not altogether happy, for they had no children.

But at last on a bright spring morning a daughter was born to them. Then great was the joy in the whole kingdom, flags were unfurled, bells were rung, and the king's messengers went forth to bid all the good people come to the christening feast. To this feast were also bidden six good fairies, for you must know there lived fairies in that kingdom; indeed, there were seven in all, but one was a dark and evil being, wherefore she was not asked to the feast.

The day of the christening came with blue skies and blossoms, song and gladness. The people thronged the palace gardens to make merry, for they loved their king and queen, and great was their joy too that a king's daughter was born. Rich and wonderful gifts were brought, gifts of silver and gold, jewels, silks, and laces. But the gifts of the fairies were the rarest and the best.

The fairies came dancing into the garden, and all who were gathered there held their breath to see the beauty and loveliness of them. All about the cradle where the king's daughter lay, they danced. And one stepped forth and whispered, "My gift to you is this, you shall become the most beautiful woman in all the kingdom." "And," added the second fairy, "you shall become as kind and good as you will be beautiful." The third fairy said, "I give you the gift of wisdom." "And I," said the fourth, "the gift of love. You shall love and be beloved." The fifth fairy whispered, "Mine is the gift of song and laughter."

Then before any one knew what had happened, the dark and evil fairy stood before the cradle, waving her wand. Cruelly she looked all about her. She spoke in a hoarse whisper. "Why was I not bidden to the feast? Ah, but you cannot escape me. The others have given their gifts. Mine is yet to come. Yes, yes, all my sisters' wishes shall come true; but when the king's daughter is sixteen years old, she shall prick her finger on a spindle and die!" And with fierce and hissing laughter she flew out of the garden. The king and queen cried out in sorrow. The fairies clasped their hands and drew close to the cradle. The mother held her baby close as if to ward off all evil. The assembled guests wept.

Then forth stepped the sixth good fairy. She smiled lovingly on all. "Fear not," she said. "Though I cannot undo my wicked sister's wish, I can change it. Our king's daughter shall not *die,* but sleep—sleep until in due time a king's son shall come and awaken her with a kiss." Thus comforted, a smile broke through the tears. "She shall not die, not die," the good folk repeated. The king then raised his hand, and all were silent. "I command," he cried, "that all spindles in my kingdom be burned!" Gladly the people obeyed, and now they all thought their lovely princess would be safe from harm.

Then began the happy life of the king's little daughter. All the fairies' wishes came true. She was the most beautiful of all, kind and true, wise and loving, and she sang and laughed through all her days. The evil fairy was forgotten.

On her sixteenth birthday, children came to play and dance with her. They crowned her their queen. They played games and were merry. But the king's daughter soon tired of their games. She left her playmates' frolic. All alone she wandered into the dark forest—farther than ever she had gone before, and in a very lonesome spot she saw a tower. She climbed the winding staircase, pushed open the door, and entered a little tower room. There sat an old woman twirling a stick between her hands, and a long soft white thread ran through her fingers.

"Good day, dear Granny," said the princess. "And what is it you are doing?" The old woman only smiled mysteriously and shook her head, as if she did not hear. "Let me try to make a thread as soft and smooth as yours," now begged the princess, and without waiting for an answer she held out her hands. The old woman placed the spindle in the princess' hand—for you must know this old woman was spinning with the spindle and distaff; and all aglow with joy at the work the king's daughter laughed and sang. Then all at once she pricked her finger—and fell asleep, and at that very moment all else within the halls and gardens and forest slept. The birds ceased their singing—the brook its murmuring. The leaves dropped off the trees, the flowers faded. The king, queen, and all the court slept where they sat and stood. In the kitchen the cook was just going to box the ears of the kitchen boy when all fell asleep. And the most wonderful thing that happened was this, a great hedge of thorny roses sprang up and enclosed the whole palace with its gardens and forests, and so high was the hedge that the tops of turrets and towers might barely be seen above it. Everything within the hedge slept.

Outside, the good folk wondered what had happened.

They tried to slip through the hedge, but in vain, for the thorns pricked fiercely, and they were all but pierced to death. "Aye, aye," they cried, remembering the christening feast, "now our lovely king's daughter sleeps, and we are left in cold and utter darkness without her." And a great sorrow filled the hearts of all.

And now and again a king's son from some foreign land would come seeking to awaken the sleeping princess, but always he failed and went sadly away from the enchanted hedge.

At last a king's son came riding though the land, and an old man of the country folk was his guide. "And tell me, my good man, what are those towers I see?" asked the prince. "And how did this great hedge of brier roses come to grow here?" And the old man told all he knew of the beautiful and gentle princess. "She has slept these many years," he ended his tale, "waiting for a prince to awaken her." Then the prince lifted his golden sword, touched with it the hedge, and cried with joy, "It is I, I, who am to awaken her!" And behold—the hedge opened—and the king's son entered. In vain his companions sought to follow him—the hedge closed again before them, for the prince and for him alone had the hedge opened. He was the prince whom nothing could withstand.

And now, within the enchanted palace the prince

walked from room to room in search of the sleeping princess. He laughed out loud when he saw the cook ready to box the ears of the kitchen boy. He smiled wonderingly at the king and queen and courtiers. But where was she—the princess? Where might she be?

The prince left the palace, and searched for her in the garden, but he found her not. Then his steps led him into the woods. He too walked into the deep dark forest until he came to the old tower. Now he too climbed the winding staircase. The door opened before him—he stepped into the tower room. And there she lay, the sleeping princess, as beautiful as when she fell asleep one hundred years ago. Her cheeks were as pink as the brier roses in the hedge and her hair as golden as the sunshine. The prince gazed and gazed upon her, and he knew that she was just as kind and good as she was beautiful. Then he knelt before her and kissed her. And she opened her eyes and looked at him. "Ah, my prince," she cried, "you have come at last. I have waited for you—oh, so long!"

The very moment that the princess awoke the birds began to sing—the flowers blossomed—everybody awoke. The cook boxed the ears of the kitchen boy, the king, queen, and courtiers stretched and went about their affairs. Then suddenly the prince and princess stood before them—and they remembered all. They had slept—slept a hundred years—and the sleep was over. "Yes, yes—she is yours," said the king, and he placed the hand of his daughter in the hand of the prince.

Then they two, hand in hand, walked into a new world—a world of bird song and blossoms, of sunshine and love.

(All requests for this story must be referred to Gudrun Thorne-Thomsen.)

BOOTS AND HIS BROTHERS

ONCE on a time there was a man who had three sons, Peter, Paul, and Jack. Jack was Boots, of course, because he was the youngest. I can't say the man had anything more than these three sons, for he hadn't one penny to rub against another; and so he told his sons over and over again they must go out into the world and try to earn their bread, for there at home there was nothing to be looked for but starving to death.

Now, a bit off the man's cottage was the King's palace, and you must know, just against the King's windows a great oak had sprung up, which was so stout and big that it took away all the light from the King's palace. The King had said he would give many, many dollars to the man who could fell the oak, but no one was man enough for that, for as soon as ever one chip of the oak's trunk flew off, two grew in its stead. A well, too, the King had dug, which was to hold water for the whole year; for all his neighbors had wells, but he hadn't any, and that he thought a shame. So the King said he would give any one who could dig him such a well as would hold water for a whole year round, both money and goods; but no one could do it, for the King's palace lay high, high up on a hill, and they hadn't dug a few inches before they came upon the living rock.

But as the King had set his heart on having these two things done, he had it given out far and wide, in all the churches of his kingdom, that he who could fell the big oak in the King's courtyard, and get him a well that would hold water the whole year round, should have the Princess and half the kingdom. Well, you may easily know there was many a man who came to try his luck; but for all their hacking and hewing, and all their digging and delving, it was no good. The oak got bigger and stouter at every stroke, and the rock didn't get softer either. So one day those three brothers thought they'd set off and try too, and their father hadn't a word against it; for even if they didn't get the Princess and half the kingdom, it might happen they might get a place somewhere with a good master; and that was all he wanted. So when the brothers said they thought of going to the palace, their father said "Yes" at once. So Peter, Paul, and Jack went off from their home.

Well, they hadn't gone far before they came to a firwood, and up along one side of it rose a steep hillside, and as they went, they heard something hewing and hacking away up on the hill among the trees.

"I wonder now what it is that is hewing away up yonder," said Jack.

"You're always so clever with your wonderings," said Peter and Paul both at once. "What wonder is it, pray, that a woodcutter should stand and hack up on a hillside?"

"Still, I'd like to see what it is, after all," said Jack; and up he went.

"Oh, if you're such a child, 'twill do you good to go and take a lesson," bawled out his brothers after him.

But Jack didn't care for what they said; he climbed the steep hillside toward where the noise came, and when he reached the place, what do you think he saw? why, an ax that stood there hacking and hewing, all of itself, at the trunk of a fir.

"Good day!" said Jack. "So you stand here all alone and hew, do you?"

"Yes; here I've stood and hewed and hacked a long, long time, waiting for you," said the ax.

"Well, here I am at last," said Jack, as he took the ax, pulled it off its haft, and stuffed both head and haft into his wallet.

So when he got down again to his brothers, they began to jeer and laugh at him.

"And now, what funny thing was it you saw up yonder on the hillside?" they said.

"Oh, it was only an ax we heard," said Jack.

So when they had gone a bit farther, they came under a steep spur of rock, and up there they heard something digging and shoveling.

"I wonder now," said Jack, "what it is digging and shoveling up yonder at the top of the rock."

"Ah, you're always so clever with your wonderings," said Peter and Paul again, "as if you'd never heard a woodpecker hacking and pecking at a hollow tree."

"Well, well," said Jack, "I think it would be a piece of fun just to see what it really is."

And so off he set to climb the rock, while the others laughed and made game of him. But he didn't care a bit for that; up he climbed, and when he got near the top, what do you think he saw? Why, a spade that stood there digging and delving.

"Good day!" said Jack. "So you stand here all alone, and dig and delve!"

"Yes, that's what I do," said the spade, "and that's what I've done this many a long day, waiting for you."

"Well, here I am," said Jack again, as he took the spade and knocked it off its handle, and put it into his wallet, and then down again to his brothers.

"Well, what was it, so rare and strange," said Peter

and Paul, "that you saw up there at the top of the rock?"

"Oh," said Jack, "nothing more than a spade; that was what we heard."

So they went on again a good bit, till they came to a brook. They were thirsty, all three, after their long walk, and so they lay down beside the brook to have a drink.

"I wonder now," said Jack, "where all this water comes from."

"Where the brook comes from, indeed!" said Peter and Paul in one breath. "Have you never heard how water rises from a spring in the earth?"

"Yes; but still I've a great fancy to see where this brook comes from," said Jack.

So up alongside the brook he went, in spite of all that his brothers bawled after him. Nothing could stop him. On he went. So, as he went up and up, the brook got smaller and smaller, and at last, a little way farther on, what do you think he saw? Why, a great walnut, and out of that the water trickled.

"Good day!" said Jack again. "So you lie here, and trickle and run down all alone?"

"Yes, I do," said the walnut; "and here have I trickled and run this many a long day, waiting for you."

"Well, here I am," said Jack, as he took up a lump

of moss, and plugged up the hole, that the water mightn't run out. Then he put the walnut into his wallet, and ran down to his brothers.

"Well, now," said Peter and Paul, "have you found out where the water comes from? A rare sight it must have been!"

"Oh, after all, it was only a hole it ran out of," said Jack; and so the others laughed and made game of him again, but Jack didn't mind that a bit.

"After all, I had the fun of seeing it," said he.

So when they had gone a bit farther, they came to

the King's palace; but as all the people in the kingdom had heard how they might win the Princess and half the realm, if they could only fell the big oak and dig the King's well, so many had come to try their luck that the oak was now twice as stout and big as it had been at first, for two chips grew for every one they had hewed out with their axes, as I dare say you all bear in mind. So the King had now laid it down as a punishment, that if any one tried and couldn't fell the oak, he should be carried off to a barren island. But the two brothers didn't let themselves be scared by that; they were quite sure they could fell the oak, and Peter, as he was oldest, was to try his hand first; but it went with him as with all the rest who had hewn at the oak; for every chip he cut out, two grew in its place. So the King's men seized him and carried him off to the barren island.

Now Paul was to try his luck, but he fared just the same; when he had hewn two or three strokes, they began to see the oak grow, and so the King's men seized him too, and carried him off to the island.

So now Jack was to try.

"Why waste your time trying? We may as well ship you off at once to the island," said the King, for he was angry with him for his brothers' sake.

"Well, I'd like just to try first," said Jack, and so

"Hew away!" said he to his ax.

he got leave. Then he took his ax out of his wallet and fitted it to its haft.

"Hew away!" said he to his ax; and away it hewed, making the chips fly again, so that it wasn't long before down came the oak.

When that was done, Jack pulled out his spade, and fitted it to its handle.

"Dig away!" said he to the spade; and so the spade began to dig and delve till the earth and rock flew out in splinters, and so he had the well soon dug out, you may think.

And when he had got it as big and deep as he chose, Jack took out his walnut and laid it in one corner of the well, and pulled the plug of moss out.

"Trickle and run," said Jack; and so the nut trickled and ran, till the water gushed out of the hole in a stream, and in a short time the well was brimful.

Thus Jack had felled the oak which shaded the King's palace, and dug a well in the palace yard. So he got the Princess and half the kingdom, as the King had promised, and every one said, "Well, after all, it was to some purpose—Jack's wondering."

LITTLE SCAR FACE

In a village by a lake dwelt a young warrior named Team. He had no kinsfolk except a sister who kept house for him. She was called the White Maiden.

No one had ever seen Team. The villagers could hear his footsteps as he went by, and they could see his tracks in the snow, but Team himself they never saw; he was invisible.

One day Team's sister called the village maidens to the council house. When all were come in and sat in a great circle in the council room she said to them: "My brother Team wishes to marry. He is a young man and very rich, but he is invisible; no one can see him who is not gentle and good. Therefore, if any maiden can see him, he will have her for his wife."

The village maidens were all joyful when they heard this. They knew Team was young and rich. In her heart each hoped to have him for her husband.

Every evening, then, as the sun set, some of the maidens would go down by the lake to Team's wigwam. The White Maiden always invited them to come in, and they would sit and watch by the wigwam fire.

By and by, as they sat, they would hear footsteps. Then the door flap would open and some one would enter. But the maidens could never see any one.

At the other end of the village, near the bushes, lived an old man with his three daughters. The two elder daughters were young women, but the youngest was only a girl.

The elder sisters were very unkind to the little girl. They made her do all the work and gave her only bones and scraps to eat.

But the eldest was the more unkind. Often, when she was angry, she would throw ashes and hot coals in her little sister's face. In this way the little girl's hair was burned and her face became marked and scarred. So the villagers named her little Scar Face.

Her father never knew how unkind her elder sisters were. In the evening, when he came home from his hunt, he would sometimes say to the little girl, "Why is it that your face is always scarred and burned?"

And before little Scar Face could answer her eldest sister would say: "Father, it is because she goes near the fire and falls in. We tell her not to go there, but she will not obey us."

One day in winter, when the first snow lay on the ground, the eldest sister said: "Little Scar Face, bring me my shell beads and my moccasins. I am going to marry Team!"

Little Scar Face brought the beads and the moccasins and helped her sister put them on.

In the evening, as the sun set, the eldest sister went down by the lake to Team's wigwam. The White Maiden invited her to come inside.

By and by they heard footsteps. Outside the wigwam there was a sound as if some one was dragging a sledge through the snow. The White Maiden led little Scar Face's sister to the door and said to her, "Can you see my brother?"

"Yes, I can see him very well," she answered.

"Then tell me, of what is his sledge string made?" said the White Maiden.

And the other answered, "It is made of moose skin."

This made the White Maiden angry.

"No, it is not made of moose skin! You have not seen my brother. You must go away," she cried. And she drove little Scar Face's sister out of the wigwam.

The next day little Scar Face's second sister said to her: "Little Scar Face, bring me my shell beads and my moccasins. I am going to marry Team!"

Little Scar Face brought the beads and the moccasins and her sister put them on.

In the evening, then, as the sun was setting, the

second sister went down to Team's wigwam. The White Maiden invited her to come in.

By and by she, too, heard footsteps. Then the White Maiden said to her, "Can you see my brother?"

"Yes, I can see him very well," she answered.

"Of what is his sledge string made?" asked the White Maiden.

And the other answered, "It is made of deerskin."

At this the White Maiden became angry again.

"No, it is not made of deerskin! You have not seen my brother. You, too, must go away," she cried. And she drove the second sister out of the wigwam.

The next morning, while her two sisters sat and talked, little Scar Face worked very hard. She scoured the kettle and carried out the ashes and fetched a great pile of wood for the fire. Then she said to her two sisters: "Elder sisters, lend me your shell beads and your moccasins. I, too, should like to try to marry Team."

But her sisters laughed and mocked at the little girl. They would not lend her any moccasins. At last her second sister gave her some strings of beads that were very small.

In a corner of the wigwam far from the door little Scar Face found a pair of old moccasins that her father had thrown away. They were dry and hard and were too big for her. She soaked them in water to make them soft.

She had no pretty clothing to wear, but she made herself a queer little dress out of birch bark.

She looked very ugly with her scarred face and short hair. As she went through the village the dogs barked at her and the people laughed and called out,

"Oho! look at little Scar Face!
Oho! look at little Scar Face!"

But when she came to Team's wigwam the White Maiden spoke kindly to her.

"Come into the wigwam, little Scar Face," she said.

Little Scar Face went in and sat down. By and by she heard footsteps. Then the White Maiden led her to the door and said, "Little Scar Face, can you see my brother?"

"Yes, I can see him; and I am afraid, for he is wonderful," answered little Scar Face.

"Then tell me, of what is his sledge string made?" said the White Maiden.

"How wonderful! His sledge string is the rainbow," cried little Scar Face.

When Team heard this he smiled and said to his sister, "Elder sister, bathe little Scar Face's hair and eyes in the magic water."

"His sledge string is the rainbow," cried little Scar Face.

And when she did so a wonderful thing happened. All the scars and burns faded away from the little girl's face. Her hair came out long and black. Her eyes were like two round stars.

The White Maiden then led her to the wife's seat beside the door.

Thus little Scar Face saw Team, and he had her for his wife.

WEE ROBIN'S CHRISTMAS DAY

THERE was once an old gray pussy-cat, and she went down by the waterside, and there she saw wee Robin Redbreast, hopping on a brier.

And Pussy-Cat said, "Where are you going, Wee Robin?"

And Wee Robin said, "I am going away to the king, to sing him a song this good Christmas morning."

And Pussy-Cat said, "Come here, Wee Robin, and I will let you see the bonny white ring around my neck."

But Wee Robin said: "No, no, Gray Pussy; no, no. You worried the wee mousie, but you shall not worry me."

So Wee Robin flew away and away, until he came to a turf wall, and there he saw a gray greedy hawk.

And the gray greedy hawk said, "Where are you going, Wee Robin?"

And Wee Robin said, "I am going away to the king, to sing him a song this good Christmas morning."

And the gray greedy hawk said, "Come here, Wee

Robin, and I will let you see the bonny white feather
in my wing."

But Wee Robin said: "No, no, Gray Greedy Hawk;
no, no. You pecked at the wee linnet, but you shall
not peck me."

So Wee Robin flew away until he came to the side
of a rock, and there he saw a sly fox sitting.

And the sly fox said, "Where are you going, Wee
Robin?"

And Wee Robin said, "I am going away to the king
to sing him a song this good Christmas morning."

And the sly fox said, "Come here, Wee Robin, and

I will let you see the bonny white spot on the tip of my tail."

But Wee Robin said: "No, no, Sly Fox; no, no. You worried the wee lamb, but you shall not worry me."

Wee Robin flew away until he came to a bonny burnside, and there he saw a wee boy sitting, and the wee boy said, "Where are you going, Wee Robin?"

And the Wee Robin said, "I am going away to the king, to sing him a song this good Christmas morning."

And the wee boy said, "Come here, Wee Robin, and I will give you some nice crumbs out of my pocket."

But Wee Robin said: "No, no, Wee Boy; no, no. You threw stones at the chickadee, but you shall not throw stones at me."

So Wee Robin flew away and away, until he came to the king, and there he sat on a window sill and sang to the king a bonny song.

And the king said to the queen, "What shall we give to Wee Robin for singing us this bonny song?"

And the queen said to the king, "I think we will give him the wee wren for his wife."

So Wee Robin and the wee wren were married, and all the court danced at the wedding. Then he flew away home to his own waterside, and hopped on a brier.

FULFILLED

ONE Christmas Eve two poor travelers came to a farmhouse and begged a night's lodging. Nay, said the people of the house, they had no room for travelers and beggars! So the wayfarers went on their way until they came to a cottage where lived a poor farm laborer and his wife. They knocked at the door and asked if they might stay the night there. Yes, was the reply, they might stay, and welcome, if they would put up with such as was there, for they were only very humble folk. The strangers thanked them very warmly, and entered the house. They had not been there long when the wife whispered to her husband:

"We must see if we cannot find something nice for our guests, on the eve of such a holy festival. We must kill our little kid."

"Yes, let us do that," said the man.

So they killed the kid, and roasted it for supper, and they ate and were glad of heart that holy eve.

When bedtime came, they gave their guests their own bed, which was the only one they had, and then they spread some straw upon the floor and slept there.

Next morning they all went to church together, and the cottagers begged the travelers to stay with them the two feast days, "for, now there is that good meat," said they, "you must help us to eat it."

The strangers agreed to do this, and stayed with them both Christmas Day and the day following.

On the morning of the third day, when they were to leave, the travelers thanked the cottagers for their hospitality. They were very sorry, they said, that they had nothing to give them in payment.

"Oh, that does not signify in the least!" said both the man and his wife; they had not taken them in for the sake of any reward.

Just as they were going out of the door, however, one of the strangers said:

"But has the kid no horns?"

"Oh, yes," replied the man, "but they are worth nothing."

He thought perhaps the strangers had some use for horns, and would have begged for them.

"How many horns has the kid?" asked the traveler again.

"Two," answered the man, much surprised at the question.

"Well, then, you may have two wishes," said the visitor; "choose for yourselves."

But the man said they wished for nothing save their daily bread, a peaceful life in this world, and heaven when they died.

"God grant it!" said the strangers; "we will come again in a year's time." And they went their way.

From that day forward everything thrived and prospered in the most marvelous manner with the cottagers. Their only cow presented them with three fine calves, their two sheep had eight lambs, their sow so many little pigs that they could hardly count them, and everything that had been sown, or that they now sowed in their little bit of land, brought forth a hundredfold. Thus they became quite well-to-do, and they set to work building and adding to their house, making it much larger and lighter.

Meanwhile they looked forward with gladness to Christmas time, when the two strangers should come again, for they knew very well they had to thank them for all this prosperity. Their neighbors and the village folk marveled greatly at all the good things that kept streaming in upon them; and the people at the farm close by, where the two travelers had been refused admittance, wondered most of all. When they heard, what the poor cottagers themselves made no secret of, that all this prosperity was owing to the good offices of the two wayfarers who had been their guests last Christmas, they were bitterly angry, and considered it had been as good as stolen from them, for they might have had the wishes if they had taken the travelers in. When these same neighbors heard that the strangers had promised to come again at Christmas, they begged and entreated the good-natured cottagers to promise them that when the travelers arrived they would send them on to the farm.

On Christmas Eve, at twilight, the same two travelers came and knocked at the cottage door. Both the man and his wife ran out to meet them and thank them for all the prosperity that had accrued to them from their visit. The strangers then asked if they might stay the night there, and spend Christmas with them. Yes, said the man and his wife, nothing would have pleased them so well, but they had promised the people at the farm close by that they would send them over to them when they came. They were so vexed at having sent them away last year, and were anxious now to make up for it.

"As you will," answered the strangers; "we will go over there this evening, but early in the morning we will return and go to church with you."

So they went to the farm.

A boy had been stationed at the door to keep a lookout for them, and he at once ran in and announced their coming. Both the farmer and his wife rushed out to meet their prospective guests, and with many apologies for having sent them away last year, led them into their best parlor. The farmer had killed a fat ox, and his wife had roasted it for them; so there was soup and roast meat, and cake and good ale, and old mead and wine into the bargain. They had a room to themselves in the upper story, with two large beds in it, with feather mattresses and pillows.

Next morning the strangers were up early, and the farmer and his wife begged them to stay at least over Christmas; but the wayfarers said they must be leaving, as they intended going to church and afterward continuing their journey. The farmer thereupon harnessed his horses to his best carriage. "They must not walk there; they should drive," he said.

They thanked him courteously, and, before leaving, one said to his host and hostess that they did not know what return they could make to them for their hospitality, for they had no money. "But wait," he added, "had the ox any horns?"

"Yes, indeed, sure enough it had," answered the farmer. Having heard from the cottagers of the talk there had been last year about the kid's horns, he understood at once what his guest alluded to.

"How many horns has it?" asked the stranger.

The wife, pulling her husband by the sleeves, whispered, "Say four."

So the man answered that the ox had four horns.

"Ah!" said the stranger, "then you can have four wishes, two for each of you."

And they got into the carriage and drove to the church, where the cottagers were awaiting them.

The farmer had himself driven them, and he made all possible haste to get back home again, when, he told himself, he and his wife would settle about their four wishes. He was just thinking of this when one of the animals stumbled and broke a trace. The farmer on this was obliged to get down and mend it. Then he drove on, but it was not long before the other horse stumbled.

"Ah! the wicked elves take you both!" he cried, and hardly had he said this before both the animals vanished, and there he sat in the carriage, with the reins in his hands, but nothing to drive. So he had to leave the vehicle standing there, and continue his journey on foot. Here was one of his wishes fulfilled. But he did not trouble himself much about that when he remembered that he and his wife still had three more. He could easily get as many horses as he wanted, to-

"*I only wish two horns were sticking out of your own head.*"

gether with many other good things. So he trudged quite contentedly along the highroad.

Meantime his wife was at home, waiting and waiting and longing for her husband to come that they might begin to wish. She went outside and looked up the road, but he was not in sight.

"If he were only here, the lazy bones!" she exclaimed, and as she spoke there he stood.

"Ah!" she cried, "now I have wasted one of my wishes! But how is it you come trudging along like any vagabond? What have you done with the carriage and horses?"

"I wished the wicked elves might take my best horses, and they have taken them. You have only yourself to thank. There is no luck in such cheating. It was you who said the ox had four horns. I only wish two of them were sticking out of your own head." And no sooner had he said so than there they were.

Three out of their four wishes had now been fulfilled, and the only one left belonged to the woman.

"Dear little wife," said the husband coaxingly, "now make a good use of your wish and ask for a heap of money, that all may yet be well."

"No, thank you," retorted the woman, "and I going about with a pair of horns until the day of my death!"

Determined not to do that at any cost, she straightway wished the wicked elves might take the horns, and in an instant they vanished.

Thus the farmer and his wife were no richer for all the wishes, but rather the poorer by a pair of horses and an ox.

THE FIRST CHRISTMAS

AND it came to pass in those days, that there went out a decree from Cæsar Augustus, that all the world should be taxed.

(And this taxing was first made when Cyrenius was governor of Syria.)

And all went to be taxed, every one into his own city.

And Joseph also went up from Galilee, out of the city of Nazareth, into Judæa, unto the city of David, which is called Bethlehem (because he was of the house and lineage of David):

To be taxed with Mary his espoused wife, being great with child.

And so it was, that, while they were there, the days were accomplished that she should be delivered.

And she brought forth her firstborn son, and wrapped him in swaddling clothes, and laid him in a manger; because there was no room for them in the inn.

And there were in the same country shepherds abiding in the field, keeping watch over their flock by night.

And, lo, the angel of the Lord came upon them, and the glory of the Lord shone round about them: and they were sore afraid.

And the angel said unto them, Fear not: for, behold, I bring you good tidings of great joy, which shall be to all people.

For unto you is born this day in the city of David a Saviour, which is Christ the Lord.

And this shall be a sign unto you: Ye shall find the babe wrapped in swaddling clothes, lying in a manger.

And suddenly there was with the angel a multitude of the heavenly host praising God, and saying,

Glory to God in the highest, and on earth peace, good will toward men.

And it came to pass, as the angels were gone away

from them into heaven, the shepherds said one to another, Let us now go even unto Bethlehem, and see this
thing which is come to pass, which the Lord hath made
known unto us.

And they came with haste, and found Mary, and
Joseph, and the babe lying in a manger.

And when they had seen it, they made known abroad
the saying which was told them concerning this child.

And all they that heard it wondered at those things
which were told them by the shepherds.

But Mary kept all these things, and pondered them
in her heart.

And the shepherds returned, glorifying and praising
God for all the things that they had heard and seen,
as it was told unto them.

Luke 2:1-20

Now when Jesus was born in Bethlehem of Judæa
in the days of Herod the king, behold, there came wise
men from the east to Jerusalem,

Saying, Where is he that is born King of the Jews?
for we have seen his star in the east, and are come to
worship him.

When Herod the king had heard these things he was
troubled, and all Jerusalem with him.

And when he had gathered all the chief priests and scribes of the people together, he demanded of them where Christ should be born.

And they said unto him, in Bethlehem of Juda; for thus it is written by the prophet,

And thou Bethlehem, in the land of Juda, art not the least among the princes of Juda: for out of thee shall come a governor, that shall rule my people Israel.

Then Herod, when he had privily called the wise men, enquired of them diligently what time the star appeared.

And he sent them to Bethlehem, and said, Go and search diligently for the young child; and when ye have found him, bring me word again, that I may come and worship him also.

When they had heard the king, they departed; and, lo, the star, which they saw in the east, went before them, till it came and stood over where the young child was.

When they saw the star, they rejoiced with exceeding great joy.

And when they were come into the house, they saw the young child with Mary his mother, and fell down, and worshipped him; and when they had opened their treasures, they presented unto him gifts; gold, and frankincense, and myrrh.   *Matthew 2:I-II*

LITERATURE COMMITTEE
OF THE
INTERNATIONAL KINDERGARTEN UNION
1928–30

Chairman, Mary Lincoln Morse, Chicago Teachers College

Mary Gould Davis, New York Public Library

Beatrice Hawksett, Minneapolis Public Schools

Frances Kern, National Kindergarten and Elementary College

Martha Seeling, Pestalozzi-Froebel Teachers College

Ethel B. Waring, New York State College of Home Economics

Adah F. Whitcomb, Chicago Public Library

Mary Reed Wood, Trenton Public Schools

A MESSAGE TO GROWN-UPS,
BY WAY OF EXPLANATION

Told under the Green Umbrella is presented by the Literature Committee of the International Kindergarten Union as a climax to the story selective work of the Committee lasting over a period of twelve years. In 1918 our Selected List of Stories for Children in Kindergarten, First and Second Grades was first published. In 1920, in response to many requests for a corresponding list of poems for children, the work of the Committee established in the fall of 1918 culminated in a Selected List of Poetry and Stories for Kindergarten, First and Second Grades. Again in the years 1926–28 the Literature Committee of the International Kindergarten Union devoted its time to a revision of the selected list, adding some new sources and in occasional instances stronger story versions. To the work of the Literature Committee of the past the Committee of the present pays its tribute, the stories in *Told under the Green Umbrella* are their selection as well as ours. We gratefully devote a page to this acknowledgment.

In publishing the present volume the Committee

180

members earnestly hope that first of all they and their
predecessors have been guided in their selection of
stories by children themselves. We humbly believe
that children are the only human beings fully quali-
fied to select their own stories. Starting with stories
chosen through many years by many children, we have
tried in selecting story versions to maintain the integ-
rity of the living story chosen, to hold true to the
background out of which it grew, and to seek beauty in
the telling.

The Committee recognizes that its present volume
is made up of stories that have already won for themselves an established place in literature for children.
As such, this book is neither complete nor representa-
tive. Many people who work with young children
sincerely feel that the realistic story should predomi-
nate in the nursery and the kindergarten; that the
earliest stories should be grounded in the here and now.
Many students of children are seeking realistic stories
worth the telling. Many students of literature still believe that a majority of the available real stories have
yet to take unto themselves a recognized type of liter-
ary interest, make-up, and form before they can fully
assume a place among the immortal stories for children.
Such differences of opinion and approach to children's
stories are both inevitable and challenging.

On the whole it seemed fitting to the Committee of 1928-30 that its first story publication be an outgrowth of the selective work of previous Committees. Already the present Committee has planned and is working toward the publication of a companion group of realistic stories; following this the next Literature Committee venture will be the publishing of a volume of selected poems for young children.

In the publication of its first book the Committee has met with many copyright difficulties, and because of them has excluded some stories and story versions it had hoped to include; that a copyright privilege was held to every included story is in itself a testimony to the generosity of the coöperating publishers.

In *Told under the Green Umbrella,* the Literature Committee of the International Kindergarten Union presents a group of stories for young children selected primarily because each one of them has been chosen and kept alive from generation to generation of children by thousands of the children themselves.

MARY LINCOLN MORSE
Chairman, Literature Committee
International Kindergarten Union

ACKNOWLEDGING THE WORK OF PREVIOUS COMMITTEES

For the list of stories and story versions from which the stories in *Told under the Green Umbrella* were selected, the present Literature Committee of the International Kindergarten Union pays tribute to the past Committees and Committee members:

Committee of 1918

Grace Hemingway,
   Chairman
Marietta Stockard Albion
Ada Mae Brooks
Mary Dabney Davis
Georgene Faulkner
Irene Hirsch

Bertha Johnston
Mary Lincoln Morse
Alice O'Grady Moulton
Nora Archibald Smith
Gudrun Thorne-Thomsen
Adah F. Whitcomb

Committee of 1918–20

Grace Hemingway,
   Chairman
Marietta Stockard Albion

Ada Mae Brooks
Jessica Childs
Mary Dabney Davis

Georgene Faulkner
May Hill
Irene Hirsch
Bertha Johnston
Mary Lincoln Morse

Alice O'Grady Moulton
Nora Archibald Smith
Gudrun Thorne-Thomsen
Adah F. Whitcomb

Committee of 1926–28

Frances Kern, *Chairman*
Mary Gould Davis
Clara W. Hunt
  (*Advisory*)
Mary Lincoln Morse

Florence Rice
Martha Seeling
Gudrun Thorne-Thomsen
Adah F. Whitcomb

ACKNOWLEDGING THE FRIENDLY COÖPERATION OF PUBLISHERS

For permission to print the stories included in *Told under the Green Umbrella,* the Literature Committee of the International Kindergarten Union records its gratitude to the following publishers:

Doubleday, Doran & Company, Inc., Garden City, New York, for The Race between Hare and Hedgehog, and The Straw Ox, from TALES OF LAUGHTER, and Fulfilled, from MAGIC CASEMENTS, by Kate Douglas Wiggin and Nora Archibald Smith.

E. P. Dutton & Co., Inc., New York, for the introduction to Olé Luköié, the Dustman, and the Thursday story, from Andersen's FAIRY TALES (Lucas edition).

Ginn and Company, Boston, for Little Scar Face, from MYTHS OF THE RED CHILDREN, by Gilbert L. Wilson.

Harper & Brothers, New York, for The Wonderful

186 ACKNOWLEDGMENTS

Pot, from DANISH FAIRY AND FOLK TALES, by J. Christian Bay.

Houghton Mifflin Company, Boston, for The Elves and the Shoemaker, from BOOK OF FOLK STORIES, by H. E. Scudder.

Little, Brown & Company, Boston, for The Travels of a Fox, from OAK TREE FAIRY BOOK, by Clifton Johnson, and The Fisherman and His Wife, from ATLANTIC TREASURY OF CHILDHOOD STORIES, by Mary D. Hutchinson Hodgkins, copyright 1924, by Atlantic Monthly Press.

Longmans, Green & Co., New York, for The Princess on the Glass Hill, from THE BLUE FAIRY BOOK, by Andrew Lang.

Lothrop, Lee & Shepard Co., Boston, for The Three Goats, from THROUGH THE FARMYARD GATE, by Emilie Poulsson.

The Macmillan Company, New York, for The Town Mouse and the Country Mouse, from FABLES OF AESOP, by Joseph Jacobs.

Minton, Balch & Company, New York, for Cinderella,

from CHIMNEY CORNER STORIES, selected and edited by Veronica S. Hutchinson.

Public School Publishing Company, Bloomington, Illinois, for The Street Musicians, from CLASSIC STORIES FOR THE LITTLE ONES, adapted by Lida Brown McMurray.

G. P. Putnam's Sons, New York, for Boots and His Brothers, from POPULAR TALES FROM THE NORSE, by G. W. Dasent; for The Old Woman and Her Pig, from ENGLISH FAIRY TALES, by Joseph Jacobs; and Scrapefoot, from MORE ENGLISH FAIRY TALES, by Joseph Jacobs.

Rand McNally & Company, Chicago, for Wee Robin's Christmas Day, and The Sheep and the Pig That Built the House, in THE TEACHERS' STORY-TELLER'S BOOK, by Alice O'Grady and Frances Throop.

Row, Peterson & Company, Evanston, Illinois, for permission to use The Three Billy Goats Gruff, The Lad Who Went to the North Wind, and The Pancake, from EAST O' THE SUN AND WEST O' THE MOON, by Gudrun Thorne-Thomsen, and The Flying Ship, from the FREE AND TREADWELL SECOND READER.

Gudrun Thorne-Thomsen, for The Sleeping Beauty, whose copyright privileges she holds.

Frederick Warne & Co., Ltd., New York, for The Three Little Pigs from the GOLDEN GOOSE BOOK.

The *Selected List of Stories for the Kindergarten, First and Second Grades,* from which the stories and story versions in this book were taken, includes over sixty stories. It is published by the International Kindergarten Union, 1201 Sixteenth Street, N.W., Washington, D.C., at twenty-five cents a copy; it includes suggestive story sources and versions.